"I'd nev

"You don't need to be afraid of being close to me," Garth said.

Lord, he must think I'm a ninny. I'm not afraid of him.

It took a moment for the realization to sink even further into Sylvia's mind. She checked the nerves in her stomach. Yes, she thought, she was not scared of Garth. It must be that she had just never been forced to live with her fears long enough to conquer them before. She'd never had to sit in a man's lap until the trembling stopped. That must be it.

It must be. Because the alternative—that she had special feelings for Garth that made her fears disappear—that maybe she was even a little bit in love with the man—was starting up a trembling all of its own. And this trembling rocked her to her foundations.

Books by Janet Tronstad

Love Inspired

*An Angel for Dry Creek #81
*A Gentleman for Dry Creek #110

*Dry Creek

JANET TRONSTAD

grew up on a small farm in central Montana. One of her favorite things to do was to visit her grandfather's bookshelves, where he had a large collection of Zane Grey novels. She's always loved a good story.

Today, Janet lives in Pasadena, California, where she works in the research department of a medical organization. In addition to writing novels, she researches and writes nonfiction magazine articles.

A Gentleman for Dry Creek
Janet Tronstad

Love Inspired®

Published by Steeple Hill Books™

STEEPLE HILL BOOKS

ISBN 0-373-87116-3

A GENTLEMAN FOR DRY CREEK

Visit us at www.steeplehill.com

Printed in U.S.A.

And it shall come to pass in the day
that the Lord shall give thee rest from thy sorrow,
and from thy fear, and from the hard bondage
in which thou wast made to serve.

—*Isaiah* 14:3

Dedicated with love to my two sisters,
Margaret Enger and Doris Tronstad. How fortunate
I am to have both of you in my life.

Chapter One

Sylvia Bannister checked the rearview mirror, not because there was likely to be any traffic on this one-lane road outside of Miles City, Montana, but because she had anxiously checked the mirror every few minutes all the way here from the airport in Billings. Between checking the mirror and praying, she didn't notice that the snowflakes were falling thicker and the temperature was dropping.

She was worried. She kept expecting a pulsing red light to fill the back window of her rental car. She'd asked the police to flag her down if they found out anything new about K.J. and John—anything at all.

But the window stayed dark except for the snow that gathered around the edges. The two boys could be anywhere between here and Dry Creek, Montana. And they probably didn't have warm jackets with them. Or anything more substantial than a candy bar to eat. And certainly not a map—

Sylvia stopped herself. The two boys would be fine. They'd faced tougher odds on the streets of Seattle. The teenagers were two of the gang members her center was pledged to help. She'd had such hopes for these two boys. She knew their background—in one of the deadliest gangs in the area—but she knew kids and she'd pinned some hopes on these two.

That's why, when she'd found out they had been offered money to kill someone in Dry Creek, Montana—and then had bought plane tickets to Billings— she barely had time to activate the center's prayer chain before she rushed to the airport, flew to Billings and then rented this car to drive the rest of the way.

She'd chase those two boys to the ends of the earth if that's what it took to snatch them back from a life of crime.

She looked in her rearview mirror again. She wondered just how far away Dry Creek, Montana, could possibly be. She'd driven down Interstate 94 and turned off at the exit that said Dry Creek. It was dark outside, but her headlights had shown the sign clearly. She couldn't have made a mistake. Still, she'd expected to be in Dry Creek by now. So far, she hadn't seen any buildings, and the road she was driving on was little more than a path over a washboard of foothills.

Sylvia opened the window and a fine flurry of snow blew in her face. She loved the soft touch of snow. Besides, the wet coldness of the flakes kept her awake. She was sleepy. She didn't realize she didn't have a firm grip on the car's wheel until she was jarred by a bump in the road and automatically swerved. With all the snow it was hard to tell, but she felt like she hit something. She was on the bank of an old creek bed and she needed to pull the car back on the path. She twisted the wheel, but the car spun to the right. Something was wrong. Then she realized the something she hit must have had a sharp point to it. She had a flat tire.

She pulled harder, but the red Buick was already tilting. She couldn't control it. She was going down the bank. She barely had time to whisper a prayer as she tipped. She felt a stabbing pain as her head hit the windshield.

Her last thought was that she'd freeze to death if no one found her soon.

And who would find her? It was four o'clock in the morning and she hadn't seen another car for twenty long miles.

Dear Lord, what have I done?

Garth Elkton sat crouched down in the cab of his ranch pickup and peered out his window at the Buick Skylark. Someone had driven the car right down the side of the creek bed and lodged it into a snowdrift.

Looked like a fool's mistake.

Trouble is, there weren't that many fools around Miles City. Not with the tourists all down in California at this time of year. Even drunks had better sense than to venture out in the middle of winter—and if they did, they didn't end up in his cow pasture half-buried in a snowdrift.

No, something wasn't right.

The early-morning light was still hazy, so he carefully checked the snow-covered ground in all directions. He was looking for boot marks or hoof prints. Rustlers had been hitting this part of Montana, and he'd even heard rumors of contract killers coming into the Billings airport yesterday.

But there were no prints around the car. He didn't see anything but frostbitten sage and, in the distance, the low rolling hills of the Big Sheep Mountain range. He could make out the smoke coming from the fire in one of the bunkhouses on his ranch and he sighed. He should be home with his feet propped up in front of the fire having a second cup of coffee.

Instead he'd come out to be sure all the cows made it to the storm shelter last night, and here he was. Trying to decide what kind of trouble that red car was going to be.

He studied the car. Most likely it was empty. Failing that, however, it was a trap set by the rustlers. Whoever drove that car into the creek bed knew someone passing by couldn't resist walking over and taking a look inside. Not after a brittle winter night like last night. Because—if the car wasn't empty—it meant some poor fool needed help desperately.

Well, he might as well get it over with. He reached under the seat. He'd feel a lot more comfortable with a weapon of some sort. He usually had more tools there, but all he found was one old hammer. He'd picked up the hammer in a ditch a month or so ago when he was out mending fences.

Garth eyed the hammer doubtfully. He'd heard of men who could kill someone with a dinner fork, but he doubted even they could do much with this hammer. The wooden handle was splintered and the metal was rusty. It looked like it'd crumble with the first blow. Not that he needed to worry about giving a second blow anyway if the men inside the car were packing guns. He'd be finished before he began.

Garth opened his cab door cautiously. A light filter of snow was falling and the weather was so cold, Garth's breath hung around him like smoke. He hefted the hammer in his bare hand as he walked low, gliding from sagebrush to sagebrush.

Garth half slid along the ground when he got closer to the car. The snow was cold on his stomach, but he hardly noticed.

The window of the Skylark was steamed up but Garth could see a shape. It could be a bundle of blankets. Or it could be a man.

A soft moan came from inside the car.

This is it, Garth said to himself. He took a deep breath, rose to his full height, hefted the hammer and opened the car door all in one swift movement. Garth was braced for the blast of a rifle, but not for the shrill scream that shook his earlobes.

He dropped the hammer on his toes.

"What the—" He swore until the small face in front of him blinked and then opened up a pair of eyes so blue, he couldn't believe they were real.

How in the world had she gotten eyes the color of polished turquoise? Garth shook himself. Forget her eyes, old man. Remember where you are. She could be a criminal. Rustlers wouldn't hesitate to use a pretty woman as bait. "What are you doing here?"

Sylvia looked up at the man. He was standing with

his back to the rising winter sun. Flecks of snow clung to the gray Stetson that kept his face in shadows even though it was early morning. The hat was worn and dipped to shield his eyes like it had been trained for the task. He was tall, six foot two or three she'd judge, and sturdy.

She shivered a little from the sheer size of him. Big men made her nervous, not that she ever let them see it. With dogs and big men, she needed to keep her nerve up.

He was angry—she could see that. His face was red with anger even in the cold. But then she saw that his eyes didn't squint the way a mean man's eyes would. She had become expert at reading anger on a man's face. At least her ex-husband had done that much for her.

"What?" Sylvia tried to listen to the man. She felt like she was coming out of a sleep. Something important had happened and she couldn't remember what it was. Maybe this man knew. She'd driven so far and so fast, she felt as if she was still moving. Then she felt the pain in her head and she remembered—the accident, the twisting of her shoulder, the impact on her head and then the blackness.

"What are you doing here?" the man repeated, and then paused. "Are you working with the rustlers?"

"No," Sylvia whispered. Her head was pounding. "I'm working with the—"

"The what?"

"The gang." Sylvia didn't know why her tongue was so thick. "The boys in the gang."

The pain in Sylvia's head twisted and she saw white...

Sylvia woke later to the sound of voices. There was a man's voice. The big man. She remembered him. His voice sounded like a low rumble. Then there was an old man's voice, raspy and quiet. Over it all, a woman's voice soothed them.

"She's coming round," the old voice said with assurance.

Sylvia opened her eyes. She was in a Norman Rockwell painting. A white-haired man with a stethoscope around his neck was beaming down at her. A sweet-faced woman with her hair pulled back was looking around his shoulder and beaming, too.

Behind her she saw the big man. He must not have heard of Norman Rockwell. Instead of a smile he wore a scowl. "Give her room to breathe."

"I'm fine," Sylvia mouthed the words. They squeaked out softer than she wanted so she took a breath and tried again. "I'm fine."

"You're sure she doesn't need to be in the clinic?" The big man kept talking about her like she wasn't there. She noticed his gray jacket was still damp from melted snow. "I can take her to Miles City easy enough—the roads aren't that bad."

Mention of the roads reminded Sylvia. "I've got to go." She started to sit up.

"You're not going anywhere," the woman said firmly, turning to the big man. "Is she, Garth?"

"Garth." Sylvia rolled the name around on her tongue. She liked it. Even if he had a wife. "Thank you—all of you—but I need to leave."

Sylvia slowly raised herself completely. She'd been lying on a plaid sofa in a high-ceiling living room. Huge windows opened onto a snow-dusted outdoor deck.

"What do I owe you?" Sylvia looked at the doctor. Doctors in Seattle didn't make house calls, but if one did it'd be expensive. She wondered how much cash she had with her.

"No need for that." The old man waved away her offer. "I was out here anyway—the boys had a horse that needed a look-see."

"A horse?"

"I tend to all of God's creatures," the old man said with a smile. "Don't worry. I went to medical school. Only took up vetting in my later years. Not that you're complicated. A vet could tell you what you need to know. Take it easy, don't doze off, someone to watch you—that sort of thing. But don't worry. Francis will look out for you."

"Thanks, but—" Sylvia took a ragged breath and swung her legs around so she'd be sitting normally. The room started to spin.

"What the—" Garth stepped to the other side of the sofa where Sylvia was sitting, and grabbed her shoulders. "Fool woman. Don't you listen to the doctor?"

Sylvia felt the man's hands on her shoulders. She wanted to shrug them off, to show she didn't need help. But even she could tell that without his support she'd fall over like a rag doll.

"I need to get to Dry Creek." Sylvia said the words distinctly. Carefully.

"Whatever it is, it can wait," Garth said, eyeing her. What he saw stopped him. Pain stretched the pale skin of her face and her startling blue eyes half closed with the effort of breathing. He could feel every breath she took through his hands as they held her shoulders.

When she'd passed out in the car he'd been alarmed at her stillness. He'd put his cheek close to her lips to feel the warmth of her breath. He wanted to do the same again. Even though Dr. Norris said there were no broken ribs, he was sure there were some bruised ones. She wasn't breathing right.

"No, it can't. Life and death—"

"Death! Oh, surely not," the doctor sputtered as he patted her knee. "That much of a doctor I've always been. No, you're not going to die—a concussion maybe, but that's it."

Sylvia wondered why the doctor's hands felt merely comforting while Garth's hands on her shoulders felt like an anchor. Her muscles settled into the palms of his hands and she leaned slightly. She'd rest a minute before she stood. "It's not me—it's Glory Beckett."

"You're with her?" Garth demanded. "She's the one who's mixed up with those contract killers I've heard about."

"I—I can explain," Sylvia said as she took another partial breath.

"Explanations can wait," Garth said. He didn't like the whiteness in the woman's face now that she was sitting. And he could feel the effort her body spent in drawing each breath. He'd taken off her coat when he'd first laid her on the sofa. Nothing separated him from her skin but the white silk blouse she was wearing. The material was cool and sleek, but he could feel her warmth beneath the material. Yes, explanations could wait. He'd just as soon hold this butterfly of a woman a minute or two longer before he found out what was making her so worried.

Chapter Two

Six weeks later, on a side street in Seattle

Garth Elkton figured he was the sorriest excuse for a man alive. He'd let his butterfly woman fly right out of his life and he'd been too tongue-tied to stop her. The fact that she was avoiding him at the time—and had avoided him most of the two days that she spent in Dry Creek—should not have stopped him.

You'd have thought it was his fault she hadn't known those two boys had come to Dry Creek to save Glory Beckett instead of shoot her and that Glory Beckett had ended up helping the Feds cut off the distribution network for the stolen beef that was being rustled out of Montana. He had not known those things himself. He couldn't have told Sylvia.

But that didn't ease her coldness to him. As near as he could figure, Sylvia had been annoyed with him just for breathing the same air as everyone else. A sane man would give up on a woman so set against him. At first he'd thought it'd been the confusion about Francis. But he'd told her Francis was his sister. It hadn't seemed to make a difference.

He told himself a dozen times he should forget her.

Still, he tapped his shirt pocket. Sylvia had lost a butterfly-shaped, gold earring when she rode in his pickup the morning he'd found her. He hadn't noticed it until after she left Dry Creek. He'd meant to mail it to her in Seattle, but he'd found he was reluctant to part with it. He kept hoping she'd write and ask about it. But she didn't.

He glanced down at the faded Polaroid picture that he'd taped to the dash of his pickup—he'd given Santa five bucks to take that picture of Sylvia on Christmas Eve and it was the best five bucks he'd ever spent. She'd been talking to the kids serving the spaghetti dinner that night in Dry Creek and her face was alive with laughter. Her smile had haunted him ever since she climbed into Glory Beckett's Jeep and headed back to Seattle.

At the time, he'd thought his yearning for her would fade. He didn't know her. He knew that. The shadows of emotions that had chased themselves across her face when he talked to her could be misread. But he had an itch inside his gut to know Sylvia Bannister, and he figured the only way to get rid of it was to do something about it.

He didn't have a plan past returning the earring. A man needed hope to have a plan and he didn't have any of that. Sylvia Bannister had made it clear she was a church woman and he figured a church woman would never take up with the likes of him. But plan or no plan, hope or no hope, it seemed the best way to start was to go to Seattle.

And here he was. Lost as a stray sheep on some wet Seattle street. Or maybe he was even in Tacoma. He'd dropped Matthew Curtis off so the man could do his own courting of Glory Beckett. Garth had thought he'd find Sylvia's youth center with no problem. He'd flown missions in the army with a flashlight held to a map the size of a baseball card.

But the streets here were confusing. Too many hills and detours. Too many gang markings covering street signs. Too many empty, shelled buildings with the street numbers erased off their sides. He knew he wasn't in the safe part of town and he didn't like the thought of Sylvia's center being here.

And then he saw a familiar face. One of the kids. John. The kid was half walking, half running down the street beside an abandoned building. Gray metal sheets were nailed over the windows of the building and rust outlined the doorway. Garth guessed the building used to be a factory of some kind.

Then he noticed that John's face was as gray as the weathered sheet metal. The kid was afraid, looking over his shoulder and trotting along like some lopsided chicken.

Garth pulled over and parked his pickup. He was going to call out to John when he saw what was happening. Kids—thugs, Garth thought—were coming toward John from all directions. Instead of running faster, John slowed down like it was hopeless.

Garth reached over and opened the passenger door

of his pickup truck. John could make it to the pickup if he gave one good burst of speed. Garth honked the horn and John looked up but didn't move. Garth had seen this before. Someone so scared they couldn't move even to save themselves.

Garth half swore. He'd have to do this the hard way. He opened his door and reached behind the seat for an old bullwhip he'd bought at an auction last week. The Gebharts were selling out and he'd paid as much for the whip as their pride would allow. At the time he wasn't sure it'd stay together long enough for him to nail it to his barn wall.

Now he hoped the whip would hold together a bit longer than that.

Sylvia stopped her fingers from twisting together nervously. She was sitting behind her desk in the small office at the center. The other staff—Melissa Hanson and Pat Dawson—were conspicuously absent. Cowards. They were no more prepared to chat with Mrs. Buckwalter than she was.

At first she'd felt like Alice in Wonderland when Mrs. Buckwalter had called, asking to see the center. Sylvia knew of the Buckwalters. True, she never traveled in those financial—or social—circles, but she knew they existed. Just like she knew the queen of England existed. She'd just never expected to have the queen—or Mrs. Buckwalter—for tea.

The Buckwalter Foundation was not the kind of donor that usually supported the center—in fact, they were more likely to donate millions to a Seattle museum than ten dollars to a small, church-funded youth center that needed a camp.

Of course, she'd be happy to show Mrs. Buckwalter around. She'd smiled into the phone in frozen shock. Today? Yes, four o'clock would be fine.

Sylvia wasn't off the phone for two seconds before she realized something was very wrong. She had assumed somehow in those magical minutes that someone from the staff had approached the Buckwalters about their ideas for a youth camp. The funding they had counted on had fallen through at the last minute and her first wild hope was that somehow word had gotten to the Buckwalters and they were coming to their rescue.

She realized how naive that sounded the moment she thought about it. A lion in the jungle didn't worry about whether or not an ant had funding. She didn't even know anyone who knew the Buckwalters well enough to get past the army of secretaries that fielded their calls. They were notorious for being difficult to contact.

Her fears were confirmed when she questioned the staff. No one had called Mrs. Buckwalter. No one even knew how to reach Mrs. Buckwalter.

That's when Sylvia panicked. The phone call had not been a miracle—it had been a mistake. Mrs. Buckwalter must have thought she was calling someplace else. She must have looked in the phone book under Tacoma-Seattle Youth Center and dialed the wrong place.

Sylvia took a deep breath. So it wasn't perfect. It was still a slim hope and that was better than anything else she had. After all, Jesus was an old hand at drawing a rabbit out of a hat. He had fed five—or was it ten—thousand with a few biscuits and a couple of fish fillets. If he could do that, he could help her with Mrs. Buckwalter.

Sylvia braced herself. Yes, she'd do her best pitch. She had the grant proposal. She needed to make some changes and it would be ready. Then all that remained was—

Oh, no, the office! Or more like the nonoffice. Sylvia used the room that had once been a janitor's storage room. The room met her needs but it still smelled of floor wax. She'd always kept lots of green plants around, but surely a woman like Mrs. Buckwalter would expect more to sit on than a gray folding chair.

And her clothes! Sylvia looked down at herself. Usually she wore a suit when meeting with prospective donors. But today she had on a bulky navy sweater and acid-washed jeans. There wasn't time to drive back to her apartment and change.

Sylvia took a deep breath and reminded herself what Jesus could do with a biscuit. That reminded her—yes, tea. She needed a pot of tea and some English biscuits.

By four o'clock the tea was cooling in the cups and Sylvia's glow was fading by the second. Mrs. Buckwalter certainly wasn't interested in the proposal Sylvia had managed to get ready.

"—we'd pair each teen with a mentor." Sylvia pressed forward with her proposal because she didn't know what else to do. Mrs. Buckwalter still held her purse in her lap. The purse was genuine leather and the lap was ample. Sylvia had seen Mrs. Buckwalter at a distance in several local charity events and thought she looked imposing. Up close she looked downright intimidating. English tweed suit, hand-tailored for her. Starched blouse. Iron hair, severely pulled back. Intelligent green eyes that seemed impatient.

Mrs. Buckwalter looked at the diamond watch on her wrist.

Sylvia gave up. Mrs. Buckwalter must have realized the mistake early on and was just waiting for enough minutes to pass so she could politely leave. She obviously wasn't used to this part of town. There must be thirty carats of diamonds on that watchband alone. "You shouldn't wear your good watch down here."

Mrs. Buckwalter looked up blankly. "I didn't."

"Well, it would be the watch of a lifetime for any of the kids down here," Sylvia said dryly. "We try not to wave temptation in front of them."

Mrs. Buckwalter nodded and slowly unhooked her watch. Then she laid the watch out beside the teapot. "It's yours."

"But I didn't mean for you to—"

"I know." Mrs. Buckwalter waved aside her protest. "I'm an old woman and I don't have time to be subtle. Don't know what made me think I might be able to pull this off slowly. Let me put it to you straight. I'll fund this camp of yours but I have one condition—I pick the campsite, no questions asked. If you have a problem with that—"

"No, no—" Sylvia was speechless. She started to rise out of her chair. Could it really be that simple?

"We'll need at least a hundred and fifty thousand dollars," Sylvia clarified. She wasn't sure Mrs. Buckwalter had been paying attention.

Mrs. Buckwalter nodded complacently. "We'll probably want to make it two hundred thousand dollars, plus whatever the watch brings. I never liked it anyway. I want to be sure they have the best of everything. Not that it's necessary for learning good manners, but it helps."

Sylvia half choked as she sank lower into the folding chair. "Manners?" She was right. Mrs. Buckwalter hadn't been listening. She had them confused with some other youth center. Maybe one of those upscale places that prepares girls to be debutantes.

"We work with young people who have been in gangs," Sylvia offered quietly as she got up and walked over to a locked cabinet and turned a key. She pulled the drawer open to reveal a jumble of knives, cans of spray paint and bullets. Each item had a tag. "These are only from the past month. Kids give them to us for a month at a time. We hope that at the end of the month they're ready to give up the stuff forever. Usually they do. Sometimes they don't. Either way, they know fear every day of their lives. They see other kids killed. They've all robbed someone. They need more than manners."

Mrs. Buckwalter looked at the drawer and raised an eyebrow. "Well, if you're set on it, you're welcome to add the prayer and Bible stuff I hear you're famous for—I don't believe it will harm anyone. But you're to include a proper amount of old-fashioned manners, too. I don't care how violent these children have been—we are a civilized nation and manners will do them good.''

"You don't mean table manners? Salad forks—that kind of thing?'' Now that Sylvia concluded Mrs. Buckwalter knew where she was and what she was saying, she tried to sort the thing out. Was "manners'' a code name for some new therapy she hadn't read about yet? Some kind of new EST thing—or maybe Zen something. Mrs. Buckwalter didn't look the type to go in for psychological fads, but she must be.

"And everyday etiquette, too,'' Mrs. Buckwalter added complacently. "Respect for elders. Ladies first, boys opening the door for girls—that kind of thing. Maybe even wrap it up with a formal dance.'' Mrs. Buckwalter's face softened. "I've always thought there's nothing like a formal dance to bring out the manners in everyone.''

Sylvia felt as if her head was buzzing. Most of the kids she worked with had probably never seen a dance more formal than the funky chicken. And if a boy opened the door for a girl, she wouldn't go through it, suspecting he was using her as a body shield to stop bullets from someone on the other side of it.

"But—'' Sylvia started to explain when she noticed that Mrs. Buckwalter was no longer listening to her. Instead, the older woman had her head tilted to the outer room. Things were getting a little noisy, even for the center.

"Excuse me," Sylvia said. She'd worry about manners later. "I'd better check and see what's happening."

The thud of a basketball sounded as it hit the wire hoop in the main, gymlike room of the center, but no one even looked as the ball circled the hoop before slowly dropping through the basket. The two teenage boys, who had been shooting baskets, had their backs to the hoop. They stood frozen, half-crouched, undecided about whether to run or to hit the floor as the front door slammed open.

Sylvia scanned the big room in a glance. The air was humid; it'd been raining off and on all day. Sometimes the weather made everyone short-tempered. But it wasn't the weather today. She saw the two boys in the middle of the floor and three or four girls sitting on the edge of the floor where they'd been gossiping.

All of the kids were staring at the front door. And she couldn't blame them. A large figure was shouldering its way inside. If they were anywhere else, Sylvia would say it was a bear. Or Bigfoot. But then she saw that the figure had two parts. John was slung over the shoulder of a man as big as a mountain. She could already hear the squeal of rubber as a car screeched to a stop outside.

The man turned to face the room and Sylvia drew in her breath. That gray Stetson. It couldn't be anyone but— No, she wasn't mistaken. She'd know that arrogant masculinity anywhere. The question was—

"What are you doing here?"

Sylvia meant to have the question come out strong,

but it must have been little more than a whisper. In any event, Garth didn't seem to hear her. Instead he bowed down in a graceful arc to let John roll off his back and, at the same time, uncoiled a massive bullwhip from his shoulder.

Sylvia cleared her throat and tried again. "What are—''

This time she had his attention. She knew it with the first word out of her mouth. His eyes swung to her and he took a step toward her. He dipped his hat and his eyes were in the shadows again. If she didn't know better, she would have sworn he was feeling shy. "I—ah—"

He never finished his sentence. The first bullet shattered the glass in the window beside the door. Garth didn't wait to see what the second bullet would hit.

"Everybody down," he bellowed as he dropped the whip and took another step toward her.

Sylvia looked around to be sure everyone was obeying. She was going to slide down when she knew the kids were all right. But that wasn't soon enough for Garth.

He sprinted to her side and in one fluid movement wrapped his body around her before rolling with her to the floor. Sylvia braced herself to hit the floor, but Garth twisted his body so that he took the impact. He landed on his back with Sylvia resting on his chest. Then he quickly somersaulted so that Sylvia was enclosed inside his arms.

Sylvia froze. She forgot all about the bullets that might be flying overhead. She hadn't been this close to a man since that day her ex-husband had threatened her—she pushed the very suggestion from her mind. She couldn't afford to think of that now. She had to concentrate on breathing. If she could only keep breathing.

Garth felt Sylvia stiffen. *Good Lord, she's been shot!*

Garth turned to his side. He ran his hands quickly down Sylvia's back. What was she doing wearing a sweater? Blood would soak into a sweater. Her breathing seemed fainter and fainter. And he didn't like the fluttering heartbeat. She felt like a frightened bird. He wondered if shock was setting in. He needed to find the bullet hole.

He slipped his hand under her sweater. If she was limb shot, they could deal with that later. But if the bullet had hit her internal organs he needed to act fast. His hand slid over the smoothness of her back. Her muscles tensed and her breathing stopped. He'd run his hand up and down her back twice before he convinced himself there was no blood.

"Where does it hurt?" he demanded.

A warm ember settled in his stomach. Her skin was softer than sunshine on a spring day. The faint scent of peaches was reaching his nostrils, too, and he noticed her hair. Luxurious strands of midnight-black hair were nestled near his neck. For a moment, he forgot why she lay curled inside his arms. It was enough that she was there.

"Ummmph." A muffled noise came from near Garth's heart and he realized Sylvia was trying to talk.

"Oh, excuse me—I didn't—" Garth pulled away

from Sylvia. Her skin was white. He felt a sudden surge of anger at the thugs outside that had frightened Sylvia. "I shouldn't have led them here. They frightened you."

"No, you did," Sylvia answered automatically. One of the things she'd been taught in her battered-wife course ten years ago was to be honest. "You frightened me."

Sylvia took a deep breath and looked up at Garth Elkton, at least as nearly up as she could. He still had her half-encased in his arms and she saw more of his chin than his eyes. She took another breath. Calmness was the key. "You need to let me go now."

Give a directive, Sylvia reminded herself. Be calm. Expect them to obey. Keep your mind focused. Count to ten. One. Sylvia stared at Garth's neck. Two. She saw his Adam's apple move up and down as he swallowed. She saw faint strands of hair curled around his shirt collar. Three. Remember to breathe.

The skin around his collar was a little lighter than the tan on his face. He obviously got his tan the hard way instead of in a tanning booth. Another breath. Then she smelled him. He smelled of wet wool from his jacket, and forest pine. She breathed in again for the sheer pleasure of it. He smelled like Christmas and reminded her of Dry Creek. She'd thought about him often since she'd left that little town in Montana. More accurately, she hadn't thought about him as much as she'd dreamed about him. Little secret segments of sleep that left her restless when she woke in the morning.

His arms loosened around her. "I was only—"

Garth protested as he moved away from her. He untwined his leg from around hers.

"I know," Sylvia said quickly. She didn't need to be so prickly. He couldn't know about her problems with men. Or those unwanted dreams. "You meant well."

Garth wasn't sure what he had meant. But he sure hadn't meant to frighten her.

"I was only—" Garth had rehearsed this line in his head and he had to spit it out. "I mean since I was in the neighborhood, I thought I'd return your earring."

"Earring?"

"In Dry Creek. You lost an earring," Garth patted his shirt pocket until he found the little bit of metal. He fumbled inside his pocket and brought out the earring.

"Would you look at that!" The voice came from the far side of the room and bounced off all of the walls. Even the kids instinctively turned toward Mrs. Buckwalter. "He not only saved your life, he returned your jewelry. What a gentleman—and a hero!"

"Well, no, I," Garth protested as he handed the earring to Sylvia, "I wouldn't say that...."

Mrs. Buckwalter walked toward Garth and Sylvia like a general chasing away a retreating foe. Her tweed suit bristled with command. "You certainly are, young man, and I'll hear no more about it." Mrs. Buckwalter stood in the center of the room and looked down at Garth's Stetson. A small smile softened her mouth as she picked up the hat. "Quite the gentleman. A fine example of chivalry if I've ever seen one, Mr...?"

"Elkton. Garth Elkton," he supplied. Something about the way that woman was smiling made him uneasy.

"I rather thought so," Mrs. Buckwalter said smugly as she walked over to Garth and offered him the hat.

Sylvia decided Mrs. Buckwalter was going senile. The older woman couldn't know who Garth Elkton was. She had him confused with someone else. "He's not from around here," Sylvia offered gently.

"I know that, dear," Mrs. Buckwalter said smoothly.

Sylvia wondered if another member of the Buckwalter family would be showing up soon to escort their mother home. The older woman was sweet but obviously not all she used to be mentally. That must explain her bizarre fixation on manners.

"I ranch in Montana, just outside of Miles City," Garth said to Mrs. Buckwalter. He brushed off the Stetson and sat it squarely on his head.

"A large place, is it?" the older woman asked conversationally as she smoothed back her hair.

"A good piece," Garth agreed as he looked around him. Two of the windows—the only two windows in the room—were shattered. "Don't anyone go near all that glass until I get it cleaned up."

"I'll get it cleaned up," John said as he rose from his crouch on the floor.

Garth nodded his thanks.

"I'd like to buy some of it," Mrs. Buckwalter said as though it were a settled agreement.

"Huh?" Garth was looking at the glass. There were little pieces everywhere. "You want to buy what?"

"The land. Your land," Mrs. Buckwalter repeated. "I'd like to buy some."

"I'm not planning to sell any of it," Garth said politely as he noted a broom in the corner. What would a city woman like her do around Miles City?

"I can pay well."

Garth thought a moment. He wasn't interested, but some of his neighbors might be. Still, he had to be fair. Sometimes there were items in the news that were misleading. "There's no oil around there—least none that's not buried too deep for drilling."

"I'm not looking for oil."

"No dinosaur bones, either." Garth added the other disclaimer. Ever since those dinosaur bones had been discovered up by Choteau, tourists thought they could stop beside the road and dig for bones.

"I'm not interested in bones. I'm looking for a campsite."

Sylvia stifled a groan. If they set up the camp there, she'd never be able to sleep again. "Montana would never do. These kids are all used to the urban situation."

"I thought you wanted to get them out of the city." Mrs. Buckwalter waved her arm to indicate the windows. "They don't have drive-bys in Montana."

Garth had already started to join John, but he

turned back. "You're talking about a camp for these kids?"

Mrs. Buckwalter nodded emphatically. "Sylvia and I were just talking about it."

Some opportunities in life came from sweat and hard work. Others drop from the sky like summer rain. When Garth figured out what was happening—he'd heard Sylvia talk about her camp when she was in Dry Creek—he knew he wasn't about to let this opportunity get away. "I could rent some space to you for the camp—fact is, I'll give you some space for the camp. No charge."

"But it's not that easy—" Sylvia was feeling cornered. She didn't like the glow on Mrs. Buckwalter's face. Granted the woman was senile, but one never knew whether or not the rest of her family would indulge the woman and let her play out her fantasy of teaching inner-city kids to use salad forks. Not that Sylvia was fussy. She'd thought more along the lines of rock climbing than etiquette, but she'd welcome a camp no matter what classes she needed to offer the kids. But not Montana. Not close to Garth. "We'd need to have dormitories—and classrooms—it's not just the land, it's the facilities."

"I've got two bunkhouses I never use and a couple of grain sheds that could be cleared out and heated," Garth persisted. He tried not to press too hard. He didn't want to make Sylvia bolt and run. He knew from riding untamed horses that it was best not to press the unwary too hard. "And it would only be temporary, of course, until you can locate another place that you like."

"We'll take it," Mrs. Buckwalter announced eagerly.

"But we have staff to consider." Sylvia stood her ground. "We've got Melissa and Pat, but we'll need another one, maybe two counselors. I can't just move them to Montana at the drop of a hat."

Mrs. Buckwalter waved her hand, dismissing the objection. "There are people in Montana. We'll hire them." She pointed at Garth. "We could hire him. He could teach these boys what they need to know to be men."

Garth swallowed. He couldn't claim to be a role model for anyone. His relationship with his son wasn't one he'd brag about. And he wasn't proud of some of the things he'd done in his life. Now that Dry Creek had a pastor, he'd thought about going back to church, but he was a long way from role-model material. Still, he heard himself say it anyway. "I'll do it."

Sylvia looked at him skeptically. "But we can't just hire anyone. They need to be a licensed counselor. Besides, I'm sure it would be too much trouble for Mr. Elkton. He can't possibly want twenty or thirty teenagers around."

Garth didn't bother to think about that one. He might not want thirty teenagers around, but he wanted Sylvia around, and if he had to take thirty teenagers as part of the deal, he'd welcome them. After all, he'd had killer bulls in his corrals and free-range stallions in his fields. How much trouble could a few kids be?

"Besides, there's the matter of the rustling—" Sylvia remembered the fact gratefully. This was her trump card. No one would suggest putting down in the middle of a crime circle a camp to get kids out of crime.

"They've been quiet for a bit." Garth squeezed the truth a little. He knew for a fact the rustlers were still there. He'd even been asked to help tip the Feds off on their whereabouts. He'd told the Feds he knew nothing. He didn't. But he knew instinctively the rustlers were still there. He suspected they were just regrouping their distribution efforts before swinging back into operation.

"These kids aren't interested in stealing cows," Mrs. Buckwalter interrupted impatiently. "Mr. Elkton's ranch is the place for them. Besides, if you wait to find the ideal camp, you'll be waiting three, maybe four years."

And in three years who knows who will run the Buckwalter Foundation, Sylvia thought to herself in resignation. It surely wouldn't be Mrs. Buckwalter. Sylvia doubted the older woman would be allowed very many of these eccentric fundings.

Sylvia steeled herself. She needed to put her own nervousness aside and at least consider the options. If the kids were going to have a camp anytime soon, they would have to do it Mrs. Buckwalter's way. And there were some pluses—the facilities were ready. She could take the kids away now. Especially John.

She knew the codes that the gangs lived by and, even though the Seattle gangs weren't as territorial as some, she knew that gangs lived and died by their reputations. Whoever was after John would want him even more now that they'd been stopped.

And it might not just be John. The kids in the center stood up for each other. They might all be in extra danger.

"Okay, I'll think about it." Sylvia said.

She didn't realize how intently the teenagers were listening until she heard a collective groan. "They ain't even got TV there," one of the older boys yelled out as though that automatically vetoed any decision. "Not in the middle of Montana."

Garth grinned. "Sure we do. Satellite. You can see educational programs from around the world." Garth grinned again. "Even get some old Lawrence Welk reruns."

An expression of alarm cross the boy's face.

"I'm not interested in educational TV or no Welk stuff. I want to know if you get *Baywatch*."

"You'll be too busy to watch TV," Sylvia interjected. She wasn't as optimistic as she sounded. Thirty teenagers and educational television. She wasn't ready for this. "We could have lessons in the various plants and animals around the area."

Another collective groan erupted.

"And maybe we can learn to—" Sylvia hesitated. What would they do in Montana in the winter? She couldn't see the kids taking up quilting. Or playing checkers.

"Skiing," Mrs. Buckwalter announced grandly. "In all that snow there should be good skiing."

The protest this time was halfhearted and the kids all looked at their shoes.

"That stuff's for rich kids," one of the girls finally muttered. "Skiing's expensive."

Sylvia hated it when she could see how some of her kids had been treated. The center served a mixture of races. Some Asian, some African-Americans and a handful of whites. All of the kids felt poor, like all of the good opportunities in life had gone to someone else. The fact that the kids were right made Sylvia determined to change things.

"We'll have enough to rent some skis," Sylvia promised, resolving to make the budget stretch that far.

"Rent?" Mrs. Buckwalter snorted. "I'll personally buy a pair of skis for anyone who learns how to ski." She gestured grandly. "Of course, that only comes after they learn how to dance." The older woman's face softened with memories only she saw. "They'll need to learn to waltz for the formal dinner/dance."

Garth looked at Sylvia. He could tell from the resigned look on her face that she wasn't surprised.

"Mrs. Buckwalter wants the camp to teach them manners," Sylvia explained quietly to Garth.

"And you, of course, can help." Mrs. Buckwalter smiled at Garth. "A gentleman of your obvious refinement would be a good teacher for the boys. Opening doors, butter knives—that sort of thing."

"Me?" Garth choked out before he stopped himself. He already knew he'd do anything—even stand on his head in a snowdrift—if that's what it took to have Sylvia around long enough to know her. But gentleman! Butter knives! He was becoming as alarmed as the teenagers facing him.

"And, of course, you'll help with the dance lessons," Mrs. Buckwalter continued blithely.

"I don't—I—" Garth looked around for some escape. Butter knives were one thing. But dancing! He couldn't dance. He didn't know how. Still— He steeled himself. He'd flown fighter planes. He'd tiptoed around minefields. "I'd be delighted."

"Good," Mrs. Buckwalter said. The older woman's face was placid, but Garth caught a slight movement of the chin. The woman was laughing inside, he was sure of it.

Oh, well, he didn't care how she amused herself. Rich society people probably had a strange sense of humor. He didn't care. He'd gotten what he wanted. Sylvia was coming to his ranch.

Maybe. He cautioned himself. He'd been watching the kids. He knew the battle wasn't over. As they'd listened to the older woman, their initial alarm had increased until they were speechless.

"Manners—" the smallest boy in the group finally croaked out the words. "We'll get beat up for sure when they find out we've been sent off to learn manners."

"We'll show them manners," John declared, standing defiantly. "We'll get them for what they've done."

"There'll be no payback," Sylvia said sternly. "We'll let the police handle it."

Meanwhile, at an early-evening meeting in Washington, D.C.

Five men, some of them balding, all of them drinking coffee from disposable cups, were sitting around a table. A stocky man chewing on an unlit cigar worried aloud. "Would he do it? The cattle rustling is only a small part of this operation, you know. He might not want to tackle a crime organization over a few head of beef."

"He would do it if he got mad enough," the youngest man said. He was on the shy side of thirty and was holding a manila folder. "His psychological profile shows he's strongly territorial, he protects his own, has a fierce sense of fairness—"

A third man snorted derisively. "That test was given twenty-some years ago before he got us out of that mess in Asia. What do we know about Garth Elkton today?"

There was a moment's silence.

The man with the folder set it down on the table. "Not much. He pays his ranch hands well. Health benefits even. That's unusual in a ranch community. He's widowed—he's got a grown son. His neighbors respect him. Closemouthed about him, though. Our agents couldn't get much from them. Oh, and he has a sister who's visiting him."

"Sister?" one of the men asked hopefully. "Maybe we could get to him that way—if he likes the ladies."

"No, the sister is really his sister," the young man verified.

"That's not much to go on."

"He's our only hope," the young man said. "We have more leaks around there than Niagara Falls. They've picked off every agent we've put on the case. If we assign another agent, we might as well send along the coroner. If we want someone who isn't with the agency, he's it. Besides, he knows how to handle himself in a fight—he was in a special combat unit in the army. He missed the main action in Vietnam— too young—but he went deep into 'Nam with his unit, five, six years later to get some POWs. Top secret. Bit of a problem. The operation turned sour and he took the hit for the unit. He spent six months in a POW camp himself. Barely made it out alive. We've checked out all the ranchers in Montana—he's the only one who could pull it off.''

The third man sighed. ''I guess you're right. We may as well offer again. Most likely he'll say no anyway.''

''I don't think so.'' A man who sat apart from them all spoke up for the first time.

The other four men looked at each other uneasily.

''What have you done?'' one of them finally asked.

''Nothing yet,'' the man said as he rose. As if on cue, his cellular phone rang in his suit pocket. The rest of the men were silent. They knew a call on that phone was always important and always business.

''Yeah?'' the man said into the phone. ''Did you get it set up?''

The man started to grin as he listened. ''What did I tell you? Some of these things go down easy.'' The man snapped his cell phone shut. Revenge was sweet. ''I've taken care of it. If Garth Elkton's anything like his old man, he'll say yes.''

''You know the family personally?'' The stocky man removed his cigar.

''About as personal as it gets.''

The stocky man grunted. ''Well, see that it doesn't get in the way.''

The man with the phone didn't answer. He couldn't stop grinning. Leave it to Mrs. Buckwalter to make the deal sweeter. He'd sure like to see Garth Elkton stumbling around a dance floor. Let him see how it felt to be clumsy in love with no hope in sight.

Chapter Three

 ❧

Sylvia stood on the steps of the Seattle police station, as close to swearing as she was to weeping. She'd almost gotten them away. If she'd taken Mrs. Buckwalter at her word and gathered the kids under her wing yesterday and run off to Montana, she wouldn't be climbing these steps now on her way to try and bail them all out of jail.

The irony was she'd worked through her resistance to the idea of staying on Garth's ranch and decided she would do it. She had no other options for the kids.

She'd take the kids to Montana she decided—at least the ones for whom she could get parental consent. Likely, that would be all of them as long as she promised to only keep them for a month. A month wasn't long enough to interfere with any government support their parents were getting for them. And they'd get permission from the schools. Both of her staff were teachers as well as counselors and gave individual instruction to the kids.

Even a month would let the kids start to feel safe. She'd learned early on that a month's commitment was about all the kids could make in the beginning. They couldn't see further into the future than those thirty days. So that's how she started. Once one month was down, she'd ask for another. Lives were being changed one month at a time.

But the kids getting arrested made everything so much more difficult. Some of the boys were on probation. A couple of the girls, too. The others had probably walked close enough to the edge of juvenile problems to be placed on probation with this latest episode. They might not have the freedom to decide what they wanted—not even for a month.

What, she thought to herself in exasperation, had possessed these kids to tackle a dangerous gang? But she knew—gang thinking was vicious. It made war zones out of school grounds and paranoid bush soldiers out of ordinary kids. She was lucky it was the police station she was visiting and not the morgue.

Sylvia swung open the heavy oak doors that led into the station's waiting area. There were no windows, but the ceilings were high and supported a dozen fans that slowly rotated in an attempt to ventilate the place. Even with the fan blades buzzing in the background, the cavelike room still smelled slightly on days that weren't wax days.

On Thursdays, when the janitors did an early-morning wax job on the brown linoleum floors, the room smelled of disinfectant. On other days the odor was people—too many, too close together and stuck there for too long.

Benches lined the room and there were two barred cashier cages on one side. The other side funneled into a long aisle that led into the main part of the police station. Sylvia's friend, Glory Beckett, worked as a police sketch artist and her workroom was down that hall and off the main desk area.

Sylvia started in that direction.

Glory might know a shortcut to get the kids out. The two of them had worked the system before. Sylvia said a quick prayer that Glory would be in her office. Yesterday morning Glory had called, worried about having dinner last night with Matthew Curtis, the minister who'd come to Seattle from Dry Creek to ask—Sylvia sincerely hoped—Glory to marry him. In Sylvia's opinion, it was about time. Glory hadn't been herself since they'd come back from Dry Creek after Christmas.

The door to Glory's workroom was closed and a note had been taped to the front of it. "She'll be in later today—try back again. The Captain."

Well, Sylvia thought, so much for some friendly help. She glanced at the police officer who was sitting at the desk in the open area across from Glory's workroom. She wondered how late Glory would be. It was almost ten o'clock now.

"Do you know—" she began.

"I don't know anything, lady," the officer said, clearly busy and exasperated. "All I got is what you see. I can't be answering questions every five minutes. You'll have to wait just like the other guy." He glared down the hallway.

"The other guy?" Sylvia's eyes followed his gaze.

The bench was at the end of the hall and a square of light shone in through a side window. That was the only natural light. In addition a row of ceiling lights burned weakly, leaving more shadows than anything. A man sat on the hall bench, staring at the brown wall across from him. Sylvia was too far away to see his face. But she didn't need to see it to know who he was. How many gray Stetson hats were there in Seattle in February?

The hall seemed far from the hub of the station and the noises that filled the rest of the building were muffled here. Sylvia was aware of the sharp snap of her heels as she marched down the hall.

Garth Elkton was the last person she wanted to face today. Correction. He was the second to the last. Mrs. Buckwalter was the absolute last, and as friendly as the two of them had been when they parted yesterday, she wasn't sure that what one discovered wouldn't be shared soon enough by both of them.

Ordinarily she wouldn't mind. She didn't have anything to hide. But this… She shook her head. She knew it would not look good to their potential sponsor to find all thirty-one kids from her center behind bars this morning.

As eccentric as Mrs. Buckwalter appeared, even she could hardly think this was a good beginning to their plans. Sylvia only hoped the woman wouldn't find out about the arrests. The older woman had made a verbal commitment yesterday. But nothing had been put in writing. Everything could change if Mrs. Buckwalter knew about the kids being in jail and had sent Garth to find out whether the arrests were justified.

Sylvia was halfway down the hall when the hat moved.

Garth didn't know why someone would put a stone bench in the hall of a police station. He'd perched on mountain rocks that were more comfortable. Not that anything about the building had been designed for comfort. Made a man feel as if he was locked up behind bars already. Guilty before he was even sent to trial.

The only good thing about the building was the hard linoleum floor. He loved the sounds of a high-heeled woman walking across a hard surface. Something about the tip-tap was thoroughly feminine. He hoped Sylvia would walk right up to him before she started to talk.

She didn't.

"What are you doing here?" Sylvia was a good five feet from him. The question could have been friendly. But it wasn't.

Garth eyeballed her cautiously. Sylvia had more quills than a porcupine and, unless he missed his guess, she'd just as soon bury them one by one in his hide. Slowly. He'd seen what tangling with a mad porcupine could do. He'd just as soon save his skin.

"Glory called me," Garth answered quietly. That much he could tell her. He wasn't sure her pride would want to know Glory had asked him to help keep Sylvia calm until she got there. "Asked me to meet her here."

Garth watched Sylvia's face. She might have porcupine quills, but her eyes were the tenderest blue he'd ever seen. And right now he wasn't sure whether they were snapping with anger or tears. Maybe both. Her cheeks were red and he noticed she hadn't pinned her hair back, instead sweeping her coal-black tresses back into a scarf.

"That's the only reason?" Sylvia eyed him doubtfully.

Garth smiled. "Well, she did tell me they had coffee here. I haven't seen any yet, but she said she'd get me a cup. Almond flavored."

Sylvia seemed to relax. "Glory does like her flavored coffee."

Garth decided disarming a porcupine wasn't such a difficult task. He moved over on the bench and Sylvia sank down beside him. He took a deep breath. How was it she always smelled of peaches? Made him think of a summer orchard even though it was raining outside and the humidity was so high that the concrete walls were sweating.

If it wasn't for the echo in the hallway, Garth would whistle a tune. He was that happy. Sylvia was sitting down beside him. She hadn't thrown any barbs at him. Life was good. Forget the echoes in the hallway, he thought. A good whistle would cheer everyone up. Garth drew his breath and then it came.

"I thought maybe Mrs. Buckwalter had sent you," Sylvia said quietly. "I thought she'd asked you to spy."

Garth choked on the whistle. "What?" His tongue was still tangled. How did she know about Mrs. Buckwalter? The older woman hadn't told him until he walked her to her car yesterday that she had a message for him from the FBI. She'd asked him again about infiltrating the rustling ring as a spy. He was going to dismiss the idea just as he'd done before— when she reminded him of the kids. The kids made him pause. Still, Sylvia could not know about the FBI's offer. He himself was sworn to secrecy. That was the way these things worked. Anyone who watched television knew that much.

"I don't know anything to spy about," Garth answered carefully. He wondered if Mrs. Buckwalter had told Sylvia. He always thought it was a mistake for the FBI to use civilians. They never knew when to keep quiet.

"So Mrs. Buckwalter doesn't know?" Sylvia said, relief evident in her voice.

Garth eyed her. Sylvia had leaned against the bench's stone back and actually appeared comfortable. Garth decided there was one advantage to the stone. The pitted beige texture made Sylvia's hair look silken in contrast. The black strands softly caught in the roughness of the concrete and flew around her head like a halo.

"About—?" Garth left the question to dangle.

Sylvia straightened up and looked at him critically.

Garth nervously tipped back his hat. He'd taken it off earlier, but then put it back on.

"If I tell you, you have to promise not to tell," Sylvia said seriously.

Garth half smiled. She reminded him of a schoolchild when she said that. He raised one hand in oath. "Cross my heart and hope to die."

Sylvia smiled back faintly, so quick and slight

Garth would have thought he'd imagined it if her eyes hadn't flashed, too.

Then she was solemn and worried. "The kids have been arrested."

Garth wished he could take the worry off her face. Taking care of some thirty kids was too much for anyone, even Sylvia. "Glory told me there was trouble," Garth said. "Actually, Matthew told me—he seemed in a hurry and didn't tell me much. He'd called from the hotel lobby before he left this morning."

Sylvia nodded. "I'm waiting to see the kids. But first I wanted to talk to Glory and see what chances we have—maybe a kindhearted judge will help us."

Quick footsteps came toward them and Garth heard them before Sylvia. "Help is on the way."

"We've got to hurry," Glory Beckett said as she rushed down the hall and stood beside Sylvia. "I've got ten minutes on Judge Mason's calendar—now."

"Well, let's go." Sylvia stood. She and Glory had been through this drill before.

Judge Mason sat behind the bench in his courtroom. On another day, Sylvia would have appreciated the carved mahogany molding in the room. The court reporter was present as well as a lawyer from the D.A.'s office.

"Just so we're clear." Judge Mason looked over a list he held in his hand and then looked directly at Sylvia. "We've got an assortment of assault charges. Aiding and abetting. You want to post bail for all thirty-one of these juveniles?"

Sylvia nodded. "If I can. I have this." She held up

the watch Mrs. Buckwalter had given her yesterday. "I'm hoping it'll be enough."

"A watch?" The judge looked skeptical.

"Diamonds," Sylvia assured him as she twisted the watchband so it would sparkle.

The judge grunted. "Doubt it'll be enough for all thirty-one. But I tell you what. I'm going to keep it low—ten thousand dollars apiece on the assault and five thousand dollars on the rest. I'm going to overlook the probation violations. You can bail half of them out with the watch."

"Half?" Sylvia's hopes sank. She couldn't take half of the kids and leave the rest.

"I'll cover the other half," Garth said quietly.

Sylvia turned. She'd forgotten he'd followed her and Glory.

"You'll need collateral." The judge frowned slightly. "A few hundred thousand."

"I've got it," Garth said.

"But I can't repay you if—" Sylvia protested. She was used to risking everything on kids that might or might not come through. But she couldn't be responsible for someone else losing money. "The kids mean well, but there's no guarantee."

"I know," Garth said, and then grinned. "But since they're going to be on my ranch, I'll have a pretty good say in whether or not they show up for their court hearing."

"Which will be six weeks from now," the judge said. He peered over his glasses at Sylvia. "I know how you feel about these kids. We've covered that ground before. I don't need to tell you how important it is that they are back here for court."

"I know." Sylvia felt the rubber band inside of her relax.

"And get them out to that ranch in Montana as soon as you can," the judge said as he stood. He then turned and left the room.

"Thank you." Sylvia turned to Garth. "I can't thank you enough."

"Well, jail is no place for kids," Garth muttered.

"And you—" Sylvia turned to Glory.

Glory just smiled. "I'd best get back to work."

Sylvia looked more closely at her friend. Glory looked different. Her auburn hair was loose and flowing, instead of pulled back. But that wasn't everything. Then Sylvia realized what it was. Glory was happy. Beaming, in fact.

"Have a nice evening last night?" Sylvia asked cautiously. Yesterday, when she'd talked to Glory about her date with Matthew Curtis, Glory had been grim.

"Mmm-hmm," Glory said, lifting her hand to sweep back her hair.

"A diamond!" Sylvia saw what her friend was flaunting. "You're engaged!"

Glory laughed with glee and nodded.

"Oh, my!" Sylvia reached up and hugged her friend. "Congratulations!"

"Finally," Garth muttered. "Glad to see he had the nerve."

"Nerve?" Glory looked over at Garth, puzzled. "Why would he need nerve?"

Garth snorted. That's how much women knew about the whole business.

Chapter Four

The leather work gloves on Garth's hands were stiff from the cold. He was twisting a strand of barbed wire to see exactly where the cut had been made. Not that it made much difference. This time the rustlers had succeeded. His crew counted twenty cows missing.

"Might be they'll show up on the other side of the Big Sheep," Jess, one of his new hands, offered. Jess was nearing sixty, too old to be out riding the range in most outfits, but Garth had hired him five months ago, after all the other big outfits had turned the man down. In Garth's eyes, every man deserved the right to prove himself, and Garth assigned him to light duty in the calving barn. Jess had been pointedly grateful ever since.

"They must have hit last night and it's already late afternoon. I should have been paying more attention," Garth muttered as he pulled his Stetson down farther. The air around him was so cold it hung like smoke. A wet frost had hit last night and the barbed wire had stayed iced all day. Garth had thought he was safe from the rustlers in weather like this. The thieves must be desperate to get back into operation if they'd work in this cold.

"You can't check all your fences every day," Jess protested loyally. "Not with the land you have. No, you couldn't have known."

Garth grunted. He'd never know if he could have known or not. He wasn't concentrating like normal on business at hand. For the past two days he'd thought of little else but the camp he had promised to Sylvia. The bubble of euphoria—that Sylvia was coming to his ranch—had slowly deflated as he drove back to Montana.

No, he'd given almost no thought to his cattle. He had bigger worries. He had a three-day head start. What was he going to do with thirty teenagers? And, worse yet, what was he going to do with Sylvia?

He'd assigned every hand on his place something to clean and he'd put his sister Francis in charge of the inspections. He missed his son, but the boy had gone to Chicago to visit an old friend. Garth wished his son were here to help keep the men happy. Except for Jess, the men had all threatened to quit. They said they'd hired on to ride herd on cattle, not scrub walls. Even after Garth promised them a bonus, they still muttered. But they cleaned—cowboy-style—using a broom like a shovel and a rag like a whip.

Francis insisted they use ammonia and now the whole ranch smelled of it. Garth took a cautious whiff of his hand. Even through the glove he could still smell the stuff. The one good thing about it all was that Francis brightened considerably as she took to her task. She'd still not told Garth what was troubling her and he knew better than to push. But it was good to have his sister smiling again, and she'd promised to extend her visit until summer.

Sound traveled clearly on a crisp cold afternoon and Garth heard the rumble of a load-pulling engine before he saw the bus crawl over the hill that led to the main house.

"We best get back," Garth said as he walked over to the horses. Garth put his leg into the stirrup and lifted himself up. "We've got company."

Sylvia stood in the long wood-frame building. So this was the bunkhouse. Late-afternoon shadows filled the corners but she didn't turn on the overhead light. She could see what she needed to see. The plank floor was unpolished and smooth from years of wear. The small row of windows were half covered with frost and they lacked curtains. Eight cots were lined against each of the long sides of the building.

Puffs of heat came toward her, fighting the cold air. Metal grates along the wall indicated gas heating, but most of the heat seemed to be coming from a potbelly stove near the door. The stove door was closed but the bright glow of a steady fire shone through the door cracks. But as cozy as the inside of the bunkhouse was, the view out the windows of the afternoon sun reflecting off the snow-capped mountains was breathtaking. The girls would like it. They might not admit to it, but they would like it. She could hear the girls now, chattering as they walked to the ranch house from the rented bus.

Above the voices of the teenagers, she could hear Mrs. Buckwalter's deep laugh. Sylvia had to give the older woman credit. She hadn't just written a check. She'd spent hours shopping and packing for their camp. Finally, she had confidently asked if she could ride with them to camp. Sylvia would have refused, but she could use an extra adult on the trip, especially since Mrs. Buckwalter had a quelling influence on the rowdy teenagers. No one misbehaved around Mrs. Buckwalter; whether it was the promise of new skis or the fact that the older woman formally called each of the kids by their full name, Sylvia did not know.

Sylvia, herself, kept watching the woman cautiously, half expecting something to happen that would cause Mrs. Buckwalter's generous enthusiasm to disappear. Surely one of the woman's relatives would step up and say Mrs. Buckwalter wasn't competent to donate large sums of money. That was one reason Sylvia was glad to be away from Seattle. She doubted any of the accountants would bother with them when they were so far away.

Mrs. Buckwalter had made all the arrangements. The bus had been rented for a month even though the driver would fly back to Seattle once the suitcases were unloaded. The driver would return and drive them back when they were ready to go.

Sylvia looked around the bunkhouse again, reassuring herself that she had made the right decision. She had excused herself from the others, saying she needed to change her blouse. She had spilled coffee on it this morning, but the small spot wouldn't ordinarily stop her. No, she wanted a few minutes alone to gather her thoughts before she faced Garth again.

She remembered being in Garth's house that morning when he'd found her half-frozen and had brought her to his ranch. She could almost picture where he must be sitting now. He'd have his boots off and his feet propped up in front of the fireplace. Garth hadn't come to the door when the bus pulled up. It had been Francis who stood on the porch and called out, asking everyone to come up to the ranch house for a cup of hot cocoa and some cookies.

Sylvia had asked Mrs. Buckwalter to tell Francis that she'd be up soon. She had thought a five-hundred-mile bus ride would prepare her to meet anyone again. But it hadn't.

Now here she was—hiding out in the bunkhouse like a coward. She shook her head ruefully as she set her suitcase on one of the chairs near the stove. Even with the stove's heat, it was still a little chilly in the room. Sylvia took off her coat and opened her suitcase. She'd be quick. Maybe she'd put on her red blouse for courage.

Garth swore as he rode over the hill and looked down at his house. The bus was parked in the driveway and he could hear the sounds of voices coming from the living room. Knowing Francis, she had everyone inside thawing while she fed them cookies. Garth hoped she kept everyone there for a few minutes. He wasn't ready to meet Sylvia. She was a city woman and he didn't think she'd appreciate being greeted by a man whose hands smelled of ammonia and whose feet smelled of cattle. Fortunately he could slip into the bunkhouse and wash up before he headed up to the house.

Garth opened the door to the bunkhouse.

Mercy!

Since the time he was a small boy, Garth had been taught to close the door behind him in winter. It was a cardinal rule in these mountains. Heat was precious. But, so help him, he couldn't move.

Sylvia stood there. Her midnight-black hair was loose around her shoulders. Her turquoise eyes were opened in surprise. She was even more beautiful than he remembered. It wasn't until he noticed the red start to creep up her neck that he realized she wasn't wearing a blouse. And the lace contraption she wore for a bra made him warm even though it was cold enough inside the bunkhouse to frost the windows.

"Excuse me," Garth finally managed to say. His manners kicked in and he stepped inside. "I didn't mean to let the cold air in."

Once he was inside, Garth kicked himself again. He'd obviously stepped the wrong way. Sylvia looked embarrassed and he certainly didn't mean to embarrass her. "Don't mind me. I didn't know someone was in here. I can leave. I just came in to wash my hands."

Garth turned to go.

"It's all right. You can wash up here." Sylvia spoke. Garth had fished on creeks with thinner ice than Sylvia had in her voice. "The sink's in the back."

Sylvia wrapped her blouse around herself, waiting for Garth to pass.

What could a man do when he'd done everything wrong so far? Garth walked down the aisle between the beds to one of the sinks at the end of the bunkhouse.

He'd turned on the faucet before he looked up. Hallelujah! The mirror above the sink gave him a clear view of Sylvia. Her skin was golden in the light from the stove. Her hair shone like black coal. It took him a full minute to realize that Sylvia was half-frozen. He'd seen that same stiffness in fawns caught in the headlights of a tractor.

He lowered his eyes and quickly washed his hands before turning off the faucet.

"There's lots of extra towels if you or the girls need them," Garth said as he turned around. Maybe Sylvia was shy. He pointed. "In the cabinet right here."

"We'll find them, I'm sure," Sylvia said.

Garth sighed. She had her blouse buttoned to her chin and her arms crossed.

"Anything you need, just ask." Garth wondered how mannerly he would need to be to make Sylvia smile at him. She certainly wasn't smiling now. She did nod.

"Well, okay, then," Garth said. He thought about removing his hat, but it seemed foolish since he hadn't taken if off when he'd first entered the bunkhouse. Instead, he nodded, too. "I guess the others are up at the house?"

Sylvia nodded.

Garth was defeated. He nodded again. This time he closed the door very carefully on the way out.

The sound of teenagers greeted Garth as he stepped on his front porch. He hoped they, at least, would talk to him.

Sylvia sat down. She was out of breath. She hadn't had an episode like that in years. She thought she had gotten a handle on her fears about men. And usually she was all right. Her days at the youth center had helped her deal with violence and fear. But sometimes something would happen that would take her by surprise and she wasn't in control. Like just now. With Garth. He'd appeared so suddenly and she'd thought she was alone. She hadn't had time to steel herself, to hide her primitive reaction.

She wondered if he knew she had been paralyzed. She hoped not. It wasn't his fault she'd had bad experiences with men and violence. And she didn't want to hear his apology or, worse yet, the polite questions that invited her to tell her whole sorry story. Sylvia reached into her suitcase and brought out her Bible.

She sought the comfort of Psalm 91. The psalm had been with her for years and it always served to anchor her. "He is my refuge and my fortress: my God; in him will I trust." She repeated the verse. The familiar words soothed her. The psalmist was right. God was her fortress. She relied on that fact every day of her life. She hid herself in the folds of His love. He protected her. There was no other way she could have taken her fear of violence and used it to start erasing violence in the lives of the kids who came to the center.

But lately she had begun to wonder if she could continue living in that fortress. She was safe, but she was also alone. She knew God would not want her fear to be a prison. She closed her eyes in weariness. *Dear Lord, show me how not to be so afraid. Show me how to stop my fears.*

Tiny flakes of snow were falling by the time Sylvia stepped out of the bunkhouse to walk to the main house. She'd put several pieces of wood in the bunkhouse stove. It was almost dark outside even though it must not have been later than six o'clock.

Snowflakes settled on Sylvia's cheeks as she lifted her face in the early-night sky. She'd never seen darkness fall like this in Seattle—a blanket of thick gray covered the sky. No stars sparkled. No moon dipped in the sky. When night fell completely it would be deep black. She was glad the camp could start in the winter. It was a lovely time of year here.

Squares of golden light showed the windows of the main house. Sylvia heard the hum of voices before she climbed the steps to the house.

"Sylvia!" Francis opened the large, oak door before Sylvia had a chance to knock. The woman was wearing a denim skirt and tennis shoes. She had a dish towel draped over her shoulder and a plate of cookies in one hand. The smell of fresh-baked oatmeal cookies mixed with the soothing smell of real wood burning in the fireplace. "Come in. You must be frozen! I was just going to send Garth down to check on you. I just turned the gas heat on this afternoon. I wasn't sure you'd be here tonight. It's too cold—"

"There's a fire going," Sylvia protested as she shook the snow off her hair. She looked around the room. Francis looked as friendly as she remembered. The teenagers were grouped around something in the dining room. A few squeals from the girls told Sylvia she wouldn't get their attention soon. "It will be fine—"

"I don't want the girls to be uncomfortable," Francis said worriedly. She put the plate of cookies down on a small table near the door. "I know how girls like nice things."

"They like cookies even better," Sylvia said. She doubted the kids had had homemade cookies in years. Most of their mothers worked long hours. Cookies were a luxury.

"You'll have one?" Francis offered the plate. "I haven't made any since Tavis—that's Garth's son— is away. I put in extra raisins. Kids generally like raisins."

"Thank you." Sylvia took a cookie. "And thank you for the warm welcome. You've gone to so much extra trouble."

"I've been looking forward to everyone coming since Garth first called."

"And you've been busy. I saw that all the cots were made up."

Francis smiled. "We worked on the girls' bunk-house first. I had Garth do some rewiring so they have more outlets for blow-drying their hair, and he even put in a telephone that goes between the bunkhouse and here.''

''A telephone?'' Sylvia said in surprise.

''I told Garth you might feel more comfortable that way.'' Francis looked more relaxed than she had in December when Sylvia had lain unconscious on the living room sofa. ''That way, when you're in the house with us, you'll be able to call down and see that everything's all right. That is—'' Francis looked shy ''—I'm hoping you'll stay in the house with us. I told Garth he was to ask you. We have so much to plan—with Glory's wedding and all—''

''Wedding! The last I talked to Glory, they were going to go to a justice of the peace.''

''Oh, not for our angel! Well, they are going to a justice for the wedding, but not for the reception. Not with Mrs. Hargrove around.'' Francis smiled. ''When they said they didn't have patience for the details, Mrs. Hargrove told them she'd organize it all for them—this Saturday night. The whole town is in on it. I'm baking the wedding cake and you're to be the maid of honor.'' Francis hesitated. ''I know you haven't had a chance to talk to Glory since you've been driving here, but she told Mrs. Hargrove you were the one she wants to stand beside her when they repeat their vows here. I'm to help make you a dress—so you see, you need to stay in the house with us. I told Garth he was to insist.''

''Oh, I couldn't—'' Sylvia bit off her words. Garth hadn't mentioned anything to her earlier about staying in the house. He might not want her there. They were renters, after all. Not guests. "I couldn't leave the girls alone."

"But with the phone you can call anytime," Francis protested, the disappointment evident in her voice. "And later when you hire more camp counselors."

"Oh, I decided not to hire any more camp counselors. I couldn't find any before I left Seattle, and Pat and Melissa thought they could handle it if I pitch in for the evening shift."

"Nonsense." The booming voice came from the side. Sylvia had not seen Mrs. Buckwalter walk up to them. "There's no reason for you to pitch in. Go ahead and stay in the house. I daresay Francis would like the company. Besides, I was talking to Jess here—" she jabbed an elbow in the direction of the old cowboy who stood beside her with his hat in his hands. "Seems the young people in this town need more jobs. A couple of them would do good crowd control for you. If we don't have enough money to cover it, I'll phone Seattle and ask for more."

That was the one thing Sylvia didn't want Mrs. Buckwalter to do. "There's no need to bother the foundation. I'm sure we can pay them with what we have."

Mrs. Buckwalter nodded. "Robert's still in Europe anyway."

Sylvia had a sinking feeling. She'd never heard Mrs. Buckwalter mention a name before and she'd wondered why. "Is that Robert Buckwalter? Your son? The one who manages the foundation?"

Mrs. Buckwalter nodded.

Sylvia's feeling sank to the bottom. "He's been in Europe for a while, hasn't he?"

Mrs. Buckwalter nodded. "But don't worry. He'll approve your camp when he gets back. I keep telling him he needs to diversify. Him and his museums. All that old stuff. I told him before he went to Europe he needed to spread his wings. Invest in the future not the past, I said. I'm sure he'll love this camp of yours."

Sylvia wished she was as optimistic.

"The Evans girl would make a good counselor," Jess interrupted nervously. "She and Duane Edison have done all right with their restaurant in town— even if it is only spaghetti and hamburgers—but they need more if they're going to buy that farm."

"Linda's perfect," Francis agreed. "She's ridden herd on a couple of younger brothers ever since she was twelve. You wouldn't go wrong with her. She'll let the kids get away with just enough so they think they're having fun without getting into trouble."

"We'd really only need someone nights," Sylvia said. "She might not want that."

Francis shrugged. "Sounds perfect. Then she can keep the restaurant open days."

"She'd have to meet the girls first," Sylvia said. The fourteen girls who had come with her all had good hearts. She'd swear to it. But they also had rough edges and even rougher tongues. If they didn't like a staff person, they could make the person's life miserable.

"I'll call her now and see when she can come

over,'' Francis said as she headed for the telephone on the stand by the sofa.

A snort of half-suppressed laughter drew Sylvia's attention back to the knot of teenagers packed into the room off the living room. Sylvia remembered that room as being Garth's office, but she must be wrong.

''Yeah, Croc—yeah, Croc—'' A simple yell grew in proportion along with some foot stomping and whistling.

''Garth must be ahead,'' Mrs. Buckwalter said complacently.

''But what—'' Sylvia started to walk toward the room.

Mrs. Buckwalter followed. ''They call him Croc after that Australian man.''

''But Garth's not Australian.'' Sylvia paused at the threshold to the room and looked back at Mrs. Buckwalter.

''It's the whip,'' the older woman confided. ''The boys are quite taken with it.''

''Surely he doesn't have that whip in there!'' Sylvia had to press her way through teenage bodies to get inside the room. If Garth was teaching those boys how to whip the hide off of something, she'd whip *his* hide. They didn't need to learn more violent ways to fight. They needed to learn—

''—sewing!'' Sylvia was dumbfounded. Garth and Trong, an undersize Vietnamese boy who was the quietest of the bunch that had come with her, each sat on a straight-back chair. Each held a needle in one hand and a shirt in the other. She'd swear they were sewing buttons on the shirts. ''Buttons?''

"Trong had a button missing," Mrs. Buckwalter quietly announced as though that explained everything.

Sylvia was speechless. A button missing! She'd go crazy if she worried about missing buttons on shirts. She was lucky to get the kids into neutral, nongang clothes. Buttons were the least of her worries.

"Garth bet Trong he could sew on a button faster than Trong could," one of the teenager boys standing nearby told Sylvia. "So we took bets."

"Not for money, I hope," Sylvia said sternly. She had a strict rule against betting for money.

"'Course not," the boy said indignantly. "We set it up boys against girls—losers do dishes for a week."

"Well, then—" Sylvia looked around. Every face was focused on the contest, except for... Some woman's intuition told her that several of the older girls weren't watching the buttons as closely as the boys were.

Sylvia looked again at the scene before her. She couldn't blame the girls. What grown man would take his shirt off in the presence of teenage girls and not expect them to notice the way the light shone on his chest, casting him in subtle shades of golden brown? How could he expect them not to notice the tiny ripple in his muscles as his fingers moved the needle furiously in and out? Or the way the strength in his back would remind any woman of those old sculptures of Native American warriors riding a stallion off to battle?

Sylvia was going to call a halt to the contest when she noticed Garth was watching Trong intently. The boy was biting his tongue in concentration as he worked to pull the needle through the shirt fabric and then dip down to poke the needle through again. Sylvia noted that Garth, without being obvious, was pacing his needle stabs to match Trong's.

Sylvia let the contest continue for Trong's sake. The boy had always been quiet at the center, as though he were still measuring the worth of the people there. He'd been pushed into a gang by older brothers, and the center had become a refuge for him.

Trong's parents had emigrated from Vietnam after the war and had moved to a Vietnamese neighborhood in Tacoma. Sylvia had often prayed for Trong, asking God to show her how to win his trust. She'd been surprised when his mother had signed the permission slip Sylvia had had to obtain from all the parents for this trip.

A cheer filled the little room as Garth and Trong brought the needle up for the last time. It took a moment for the boys and girls to look at each other suspiciously.

"We won." One of the girls claimed the moment. "Garth finished first."

"Did not," one of the boys declared defiantly. "Trong's our man and he pulled his needle out first."

"Trong. Trong." The boys started to chant. "He's our man. Trong."

The Vietnamese boy looked at the floor, but Sylvia could see a smile on his lips. Victory was sweet for the boy.

"But we won," one of the girls said, looking up at Garth for confirmation.

"I think I was just a little bit slower than Trong here," Garth said. But then he flashed a smile at the girls. "Don't worry, though. I'll help you with the dishes."

Sylvia could see the girls exchange hesitant glances. It was clear that the thought of Garth helping them with the dishes made the defeat more than bearable.

"Okay, then," several of the girls said, and one added, "But you do the pots and pans."

"Gladly," Garth agreed as he stood and slipped his arms into the sleeves of his shirt.

Sylvia almost groaned. She'd planned on struggling with finances on this trip. And quarreling teenagers. And cold weather. And plain food, if necessary. But she'd not come expecting the inevitable crushes it looked like Garth would inspire.

Lord have mercy on them all.

Chapter Five

It was only nine o'clock in the morning and Garth was tired. Bone-weary, butt-dragging tired. He hadn't been this tired after riding rodeo in Miles City last summer.

No, he thought to himself as he hid out in the barn, this kid-rearing stuff would wear a person out. No matter what he was doing, thirty pairs of eyes were watching him. No matter where he went, thirty teenagers came, too. He was beginning to wonder how mother ducks could stand it with all their ducklings following them and mimicking their actions. And the worst part was that he'd come to realize he wasn't a fit mother duck. He'd burned his finger on the stove this morning and—before he thought about it—he swore. Ten kids heard him. He knew these kids weren't choir boys. They could probably outcuss him. But what came out of their mouths and what came out of his mouth were two different things. He was determined to be a good role model if it killed him.

Right now he was thinking it just might do that.

And if it was going to kill him, it might as well do it now that breakfast was over.

He must have flipped ten dozen pancakes. All flipped to order—some deep dark for the guys who said they'd heard about bacteria in eggs. Others lightly seared for the group that didn't like them crusty. Half of them with bacon strips enfolded in the middle. He was thankful Sylvia had sense enough to put her foot down about eggs—the eggs were scrambled. Take them as you get them or not at all.

A slow grin spread over Garth's face as he leaned back into a bale of hay. It was almost worth it all to watch Sylvia's face during the whole production. She confided in him halfway through that she'd never fixed a meal for all the kids before. He nodded like he wouldn't have known if she hadn't told him. But it was obvious. Sylvia was as unprepared as he was. The kids ate more than the branding crew he fed each fall. He would have suspected they'd gotten up in the middle of the night for a game of football, but the snow was smooth on the ground. They must just eat this much. It was an alarming thought.

"It'll be macaroni and cheese for lunch," Sylvia whispered frantically as she stirred another pan of scrambled eggs. "Out of a box."

"Too many carbohydrates," Mrs. Buckwalter objected. The older woman had decided not to leave with the bus driver when he left late last night. This morning she'd tied a towel around her dress and was frying her seventh pan of bacon.

"We have a bag of apples," Garth offered. "Give

them some raw carrots and an apple and they'll be set.''

"Makes them sound like horses,'' Sylvia protested.

"They eat like horses!''

Mrs. Buckwalter grunted. "Maybe by dinner I can call my chef back home and get a big recipe for something stir-fried.''

"Can't stir-fry for this many people,'' Sylvia said as she scooped the scrambled eggs into a bowl and handed it to a waiting teenager. "Not unless you've got a big wok.''

Mrs. Buckwalter looked at Garth. He shook his head and shrugged. "Sorry.''

"Well, surely people have something for crowds this big.'' Mrs. Buckwalter reached up to wipe a thin sheen of sweat off her forehead. She was beginning to look a little frantic herself. "I wonder if my chef could deliver something—you know like florists do— you order local and someone else delivers. Let your fingers do the cooking—that sort of thing.''

"We'll think of something.'' Garth soothed the older woman. "I can always make hamburgers—'' he flexed his hand and grimaced "—I'm just getting the flipping down.''

"We vote for hamburgers,'' one of the girls said as a group of them held out their plates for more pancakes. "And paper plates so there'll be no cleanup.''

Dishes. Garth groaned inside. The cooking was only the beginning. Then he needed to help with dishes. "Dishes will be fun.'' He tried to sound enthusiastic. "Lots of fun.''

The girls giggled as they accepted their pancakes and walked back to the tables Francis had set up in the living room.

Garth was proud of himself for managing to be a good role model. He'd been giving some thought to what Matthew had told him about living the Christian life. Matthew insisted grace was the way to heaven. But Garth didn't trust grace or mercy. Not that mercy wasn't all right for some folks. Especially people that didn't have anything else going for them.

But Garth wasn't willing to bet his eternal happiness on something as uncontrollable as mercy. Not when he could beat most opponents by himself. No, he wasn't going to trust mercy. Not when he could pull up his shirtsleeves and work his way to redemption.

Yes, sir, he thought to himself in satisfaction. He could do it. Look at him. Not only was he flipping pancakes, he was spreading morning cheer. That had to rack up the points.

"Don't encourage them," Sylvia said stiffly.

"What—?" Garth protested.

"You know what I mean." Sylvia set the egg spoon down in the pan sharply. "I won't have their heads turned with—with—" She looked at him in exasperation. "With you."

"Me?"

Garth didn't get an explanation. Instead, Sylvia held her chin high, speared one of the remaining pancakes, tossed it on a plate and headed out to the tables in the living room.

"Me?" Garth asked again.

This time Mrs. Buckwalter answered him. Well, she didn't so much answer him as chuckle. "Ah, yes," the older woman said with what Garth could only describe as glee.

Then Mrs. Buckwalter took a pancake, too, and topping it off with three hot bacon strips, she followed Sylvia into the living room.

Garth decided to load a plate with the leftover pancakes, all three of them. One burnt, one broken and one...well, one that wasn't bad. Then he headed out to the barn. For generations the barn had been a refuge for misunderstood men. He'd eat his pancakes there.

Sylvia squared her shoulders. She'd sat down to eat her breakfast. But she couldn't. Something kept nagging at her and nagging at her. She'd driven a man out of his home. He hadn't even bothered to put on a heavy coat and it was cold outside. That Stetson he wore wouldn't keep his ears warm, either. Sometimes, she thought, treating others like yourself could be a tiresome business. She owed him an apology. He did seem unaware of the crushes he was inspiring. Perhaps he was innocent.

Never let it be said, she told herself as she stood, that she had falsely accused someone and not had the personal fortitude to apologize for it.

"I'm sorry." She said the words into the empty air of the barn. She said them loudly and clearly so there would be no need to tarry. A good clean apology and she would be done with it and back to her breakfast.

Giving an apology, unlike firing a musket, did not require one to see the white of an enemy's eyes.

She knew Garth was in the barn someplace. She'd just seen him enter, carrying a plate. Still, she looked into the shadows. The barn did not have windows. The only light came from the huge, cut-out door that swung up from the barn's side like a garage door. Bales of straw were stacked in one corner of the barn, next to a series of stalls. A trough of water, with a faucet at one end, stood against the far side of the barn. The sunlight filtered into the gray shadows. The straw was musty and made the air heavy, almost warm.

The only response Sylvia got to her apology was a grunt from somewhere in the bowels of the barn.

"I said I was sorry," she repeated. There, she'd said it twice. That should certainly be enough.

The grunt this time sounded closer.

"You shouldn't eat out here anyway. There could be rats."

"Rats!"

A form moved in the shadows and walked indignantly toward her, carrying a plate. "There's no rats in my barn! I keep a clean barn. Look around."

"All I meant was that you should eat inside—with people."

Garth stepped out of the shadows and smiled. "Are you inviting me to have breakfast with you?"

Garth had pushed his Stetson back and she could see his eyes. Warm brown eyes that teased. His cheeks were freshly shaved and the collar of his shirt was crisply ironed.

But it was the smile that held her gaze. Sylvia wasn't sure about that smile. Just this morning she'd seen a cat with that expression looking at a bowl of new cream after Francis brought the milk to the house.

"Well, no, not *me*—" Sylvia spread her hands. "You should have breakfast with us—the people here."

"Eating breakfast with thirty teenagers isn't my idea of the best way to start a day."

Sylvia decided she had done enough. She turned to leave. "Suit yourself. Be a hermit."

Unfortunately, Garth thought, even hermits have to do dishes. Especially when they'd promised fourteen young girls they'd help.

"I got soap in my eyes!" One of the girls tugged at Garth's arm. "Look at my eyes."

Garth looked down into the girl's eyes. They didn't look red, but maybe the soap hadn't had time to settle in yet. "Blink, and then we'll rinse them with cold water."

Garth was up to his elbows in hot water and suds. He was tackling the frying skillets from breakfast and the plates. The silverware was soaking in a tub and the girls were washing the cups and glasses.

He hadn't realized washing dishes was such a perilous task until everyone started getting soap in their eyes. He was beginning to wonder if they shouldn't do away with the soap and just sterilize the dishes in scalding water. Maybe he could rig up some kind of a hose and they could put the dishes outside while they sterilized them.

"I've got soap, too," another girl wailed just as Sylvia entered the kitchen.

Garth looked down at a pair of wide brown eyes. He took longer this time. He'd just as soon look at the girl's eyes as look at what his heart wanted him to see.

Sylvia had been outside, and when she entered the kitchen she unwrapped a red wool scarf from around her head. The static from the wool made her hair swirl around her in tender tiny strands. They softened her face until she looked young and vulnerable. The cold had made her cheeks—and her nose—pink. The pink in her cheeks made her blue eyes stand out even more. She was adorable.

And Garth knew he dared not look at her. If he did, his eyes might reveal the feelings churning inside him. He didn't know Sylvia well, but he knew her well enough to know he needed to go slow with her. She wasn't ready for the sledgehammer of emotions that were hitting at him.

"Your eyes look fine to me," Garth finally said instead to the girl. "Maybe it was just a little speck of soap."

"I think the girls have helped enough," Sylvia said as she took off her coat and hung it on a peg by the door. "Pat is waiting for them before he starts the math lessons."

The girls groaned, but they obediently folded their dish towels and filed out of the kitchen.

Garth took his hands out of the dishwater. He knew

women liked sensitive men these days—men who weren't afraid of domestic chores—but he doubted dishpan hands were considered sexy.

Besides, he had better things to do than wash dishes. Sylvia might not be ready to know how he felt about her, but he could take one small step.

He figured his moments alone with Sylvia—with teenagers in the house—were going to be few and far between. He needed to make the most of them when he had them.

"I'll let everything soak for a minute," he said as he dried his hands on the towel wrapped around his waist. The towel! That was another thing that had to go. He almost wished he had a reason to bring out the leather chaps he used for roundup time. Women always seemed to like chaps. Even a man doing dishes would look good in chaps.

"That's good," Sylvia said as she walked over to the kitchen table and sat down on a chair. "I wanted to talk to you about something anyway."

Garth congratulated himself. That had to be a good sign. Maybe Sylvia wasn't as indifferent to him as he thought. He walked over and sat down himself. "Talk away."

The clock in the kitchen quietly ticked in the background as Sylvia drew in a breath.

"You're doing more for us than you need to—" Sylvia's quiet voice began.

Garth didn't interrupt. He knew this wasn't the point Sylvia was talking toward. He knew because she didn't look him in the eye. She seemed to be talking to his chin. Something was bothering her.

"—and we appreciate it," Sylvia continued.

Garth nodded. "No problem."

Sylvia raised her eyes and looked at him directly. "But I'm worried—crushes can hurt people."

Garth tried to swallow. How had she known? He thought he was being subtle. He hadn't even taken one tiny first step yet and she knew where he was going.

"You don't need to worry about me," Garth finally said stiffly.

"You?" Sylvia said, surprise adding even more color to her face. "Why would I worry about you? It's the girls I'm worried about."

"The girls." Garth knew he was slow, but he didn't know what she was talking about. The only one around here with anything remotely resembling a crush was him. And he wasn't so sure it could be called a crush; it was more like an avalanche.

"All this business of soap in their eyes—" Sylvia spread her hands and shook her head. "I know it's natural for girls their age to have crushes, but—"

"You think the girls have crushes on me." Garth was stunned and relieved at the same time. His secret was safe. "I don't think so. I'm old enough to be their father."

"Exactly. That's your attraction."

Sylvia studied Garth. He was old enough to be their father; that was obvious. He was even starting to act like one ever since he'd started cooking for the kids.

"The girls wish they had fathers like you," she continued softly. "They see you as someone safe."

"I am safe. I wouldn't hurt them."

Now that the cards were being laid out on the table, Garth found a slow, growing anger building in his gut. What kind of a man did she think he was? "I wouldn't let anyone else hurt them, either."

Sylvia smiled. "They know that. That's why they have crushes on you."

Garth felt his anger fade. "So what do you want me to do?"

"Be kind to them. But not too kind. And whatever you do, don't single someone out for special treatment. There'd be a fight for sure if you did that."

"I can do that," Garth said.

Garth finished the breakfast dishes and went out to check the calving barn. Jess had been up all night delivering twin calves. One of the calves needed to be bottle-fed and Garth snapped one of the agricultural nipples onto the bottle. While the calf sucked, Garth congratulated himself. He was beginning to think he had a handle on this camp stuff. Huge meals. He could do that. Mountains of dishes. He could do that. Treat all the girls the same. He could do that.

There was a time when warriors needed to fight each other for the hand of the fairest maiden. Garth figured he had it easy. All he needed to do was be Martha Stewart to thirty hungry teenagers. Well, that and learn to dance so Mrs. Buckwalter would be happy.

The calf sucked in the last of the milk supplement and butted its head against the empty bottle.

"Easy does it, fella," Garth said as he rubbed the calf along its back. The way the calf was eating, it would fill out in no time.

Garth sat back on his heels. Actually, he'd need to do more than just learn to dance to make the camp work as Mrs. Buckwalter saw it. He wasn't too sure what Mrs. Buckwalter meant by manners, but he was pretty sure she wasn't thinking of the country manners that said you just treated your neighbor like yourself and respected their boundaries and water rights.

He suspected, with all her money, Mrs. Buckwalter fancied manners of a different sort. He was pretty sure she'd let him slide on his share of the manners since he'd agreed to do what he could to help the FBI in their investigation. But she wouldn't let the kids slide, and since they looked to him for help, he'd need to make the correct motions himself.

Garth stood up and brushed the straw off his jeans. Now that he thought about it, he was beginning to wonder if warriors didn't have it easier after all. He'd rather face an opponent he could see. Manners were a completely different kind of target. He didn't even know whom to ask about manners. The closest thing to Mrs. Buckwalter they had around here was Mrs. Hargrove. Even though Mrs. Hargrove was plain speaking and plain dressing, she believed in style. The pageant she'd planned for the community over Christmas showed that. Maybe she could help him.

That same morning in a windowless room in Washington, D.C.

The "suits" had been called back together. The only clue that something was wrong was the silence in the room as they waited for the last man to sit down at the table.

"We've got trouble," the leader said. He tapped an unlit cigar on the table. "There's a leak somewhere—I'm afraid the rustlers might know about Elkton."

"They can't," the youngest man said confidently. He opened his manila folder as though it contained new information. "We just got the word back ourselves that he agreed to help. What makes you think they know anything?"

"Gut feeling," the leader said. "We were getting close to the inside man and then—all of a sudden—everything gets too easy. Like they want our attention diverted for a bit. I figure it's got to do with Elkton. They don't want us thinking about him."

None of the men disputed the older man's gut feeling. His gut was more reliable than their most sophisticated computers.

"Maybe we should send someone out to check," the younger man suggested.

"Can't. That would finger him for sure." The older man twisted his cigar again.

"We could send someone if they knew how to get in and out without being seen," the usually silent man offered. He'd expected another call on his cell phone from Mrs. Buckwalter saying everything was all right. But the call hadn't come. Not yet.

Just then the cell phone rang in the other man's pocket. "That'll be Mrs. Buckwalter."

The rest of the men were silent while he answered the phone. "Yes?"

The man's face went pale and he gripped the phone tighter. "Who are you?"

The men could hear the loud laughter on the other end of the phone.

"I'm not interested in your games," the man said. Nothing in his voice showed the strain he was under. "If you won't tell me who you are, I'm going to hang up."

The laughter on the other end of the phone stopped, and they could hear the mumble of conversation. Then there was silence.

"All right," the man said. "My name is Flint Russell. Now tell me yours."

The men exchanged looks of surprise. Flint was a veteran agent. He'd never give out his name unless something very serious was happening.

"Forget about the sister. She doesn't know anything." Sweat was forming on Flint's forehead, but he did not notice it. He knew he had to keep his voice calm. Why hadn't he thought about that? The rustlers were planning to sway Garth's sympathies by taking Francis. He only hoped they didn't know—

"That was a long time ago." Flint ground his teeth together so his voice would sound even. He supposed it wasn't a government secret that he had been married to Francis twenty years ago for two days. The ink hadn't even dried on their license before it was all over. After all that time he was surprised that anyone besides himself still cared enough to remember.

"Like I said, that was a long time ago. Don't waste your time taking her."

There was a sharp bark of laughter and the phone line went dead.

Chapter Six

"That's your salad fork," Sylvia reminded K.J. as the teenager grabbed his closest fork and speared a few macaroni covered with cheese sauce. "Remember, you use silverware from the outside in."

Lunch was underway. Sylvia had offered a brief prayer and then Garth had carried in one and then two more big roasting pans filled with macaroni and cheese. The ranch hands were sitting uneasily with the teenagers from the center. Everyone looked hungry. Sylvia hoped there was a recycler around for all the cardboard boxes they'd opened.

"Huh?" K.J. stopped with the fork halfway to his mouth.

Forty-three people were seated around three metal banquet tables that took up most of the living room. Francis had brought out some old linens to cover the tables and she'd called Linda to ask about borrowing fifty-odd settings of silverware from the café in Dry Creek. Linda had brought the silverware over earlier.

"Remember we talked about it after math? The forks are placed in the order in which you use them. Salad first. Then the main meal. Remember, the first fork goes with the first food. Salad." Sylvia felt a throbbing behind her eyes. She'd already talked about forks for an hour today. She felt like eating her own meal with a wooden spoon. But Mrs. Buckwalter seemed happy with the progress the kids were making.

"But I'm eating macaroni and cheese first. First fork. First food. Ain't going to have no salad yet," K.J. explained. He looked around at the others for support and got a few confused nods, mostly from the ranch hands. The working men had mended fence somewhere this morning and so hadn't seen the training about forks.

"But the salad is supposed to come first," Sylvia explained again. She knew K.J. didn't like rules. He'd grown up without any and he chafed at the simplest ones. Sylvia knew teenagers needed structure and that kids like K.J. needed it more than most. She just wished all of the rules here could be important ones. She'd rather teach them "Thou shalt not kill" than which fork to use, but she'd given her word to Mrs. Buckwalter, and the camp would teach manners no matter how much patience it took. "If it comes first, you use the first fork."

"Gonna eat my salad last. For dessert like. Gonna use my salad fork then," K.J. offered, and looked a little mournfully at the two chocolate cakes Francis had baked. "Can't have dessert. I'm not supposed to have sugar. Or chocolate. That stuff'll kill you."

"But—" Sylvia felt the throbbing in her head increase. She wondered what fork one used to eat an extrastrength aspirin.

"Maybe it'll help to remember that the big fork is for the big part of the meal," Garth suggested. He also had mended fences this morning, but it took little imagination to figure out what the fork talk had been all about. "The little ones just come before and after it."

K.J. set down his salad fork and shook his head. "Don't make no sense to me. Who cares what fork I use?"

"I care, Mr. Colton." Mrs. Buckwalter put her own fork on her plate and looked down the long banquet table at K.J. "And so will your employer someday when he takes you out to lunch to see if you've got the table manners to deal with important clients."

"I ain't got no job," K.J. mumbled as he looked down at his plate. "Ain't nobody gonna hire me anyway. Not for a real job. Not one like that where there's clients and all."

"Of course they will. You've got natural sales ability," Mrs. Buckwalter said briskly. "And when they do, you'll know you can dine anywhere and be comfortable."

Mrs. Buckwalter looked at Garth and added, "That reminds me, we need to have lobster one night."

Garth took the news like a man. He flinched but he didn't swear.

Sylvia panicked. "Lobster!" If it didn't come in a box, she couldn't cook it.

"We can't—" Sylvia looked at Garth for help.

Mrs. Buckwalter hadn't been around for the lunch preparations. Maybe she'd forgotten they were all novices in the kitchen.

Garth smiled reassuringly at Sylvia before looking down the table at Mrs. Buckwalter. "You mean some casserole dish with that flaked lobster—or is it crab?—that they have in the grocery store in Baker?" We could probably use that in one of the recipes I had in the army. Tuna on a shingle—only, it'd be lobster on toast. Fancy like. I could make that. Might be good.

"Oh, no." Mrs. Buckwalter shuddered and waved the suggestion aside. "I mean lobster. Every businessman—" Mrs. Buckwalter looked at the boys and then the girls and added sternly "—and businesswoman needs to know how to eat a lobster. They're slippery little things, and anyone in business is bound to end up face-to-face with one of them at some dinner. They need to know how to crack them and how to dip them in butter delicately."

"Couldn't we have pizza instead?" one of the girls asked hopefully. Paula was a fourteen-year-old African-American who had come to the center last fall when her father had been killed. "We could make it anchovy if you're set on something fishy."

One of the boys groaned, but got an elbow in the ribs from his neighbor.

"I can order pizza," Garth agreed eagerly. "And it doesn't need to be anchovy. We could do sausage. Or pepperoni. They don't usually deliver out from Baker, but with an order this big—"

"No pizza. Not for the kind of job Miss Smith is

going to have someday." Mrs. Buckwalter looked at the teenager assessingly. "And then again—maybe not. I see you as a teacher of some kind."

"Me?" Paula asked in surprise.

Mrs. Buckwalter nodded confidently. "Oh, yes, I've watched you helping the other kids with their math. You've got the knack for it."

Paula beamed. She picked up her dinner fork and speared a macaroni. "Well, I guess it wouldn't hurt to eat a lobster. Learn something new."

"So pizza is out?" Sylvia asked reluctantly. Maybe Mrs. Buckwalter had forgotten breakfast. She didn't seem to remember they needed to think boxes and cans when it came to menu preparation. They weren't even ready for steaks. And steaks were dead. No, they were definitely not ready for something that was alive.

"Really, it's no trouble to call for pizza." Garth tried again. "They even have those padded boxes that keep it warm until it gets here."

"Maybe we could have lobsters at the wedding reception on Saturday." Mrs. Buckwalter ignored Garth and continued to muse. "There'll, of course, be lots of dancing. And a nice sit-down dinner. Wouldn't that be just perfect?"

"At the wedding?" Sylvia gasped. They would need lobsters for at least eighty people! Everyone in Dry Creek was coming. They couldn't possibly cook that many lobsters. Someone needed to stop Mrs. Buckwalter. "Oh, but lobsters are…so big. I've always rather liked little finger sandwiches at weddings. You know you can make them with tuna or cream cheese and olives or smoked salmon. You can cut them into fancy shapes—hearts or squares. We could put them on doilies. Or if you didn't like that, we could bake those little quiches. Or wrap asparagus in ham."

Mrs. Buckwalter wasn't paying attention. She was surveying the teenagers like a general surveying her troops before she charged into battle.

"If everyone—" Mrs. Buckwalter waved her hands at the kids "—is going to learn how to dance for the event, then I say let's make it special."

Dancing! Sylvia forgot about the lobsters. She had more immediate worries. She needed to turn these teens into dancers for the big event. The kids were all looking at Mrs. Buckwalter like it could happen. If the older woman said they could dance, they would. Sylvia wished she had as much blind faith. She knew dancing didn't just happen. Someone needed to teach them.

Sylvia was beginning to appreciate the difficulty of fairy-tale endings. Take Cinderella. It was obvious that the true hero in Cinderella wasn't the prince. All he had to do was look good and carry around a shoe. No, it was the fairy godmother who had to sweat. Sylvia wondered if the poor fairy felt like she did this very minute—like she'd promised the impossible and had no idea how to deliver it.

Then she remembered. She did not have to deliver anything. She had Garth. He could teach the kids to dance.

Sylvia put the last paper plate into the trash bag. They'd used large paper plates for the macaroni and cheese and small paper plates for the chocolate cake. If they hadn't needed the various sizes of forks, they would have used plastic silverware, too. Sylvia was glad. She'd rather burn the dirty dishes than have the girls wash them. She would have enough trouble with their crushes when Garth started teaching them to dance.

"You need to rest," Garth said as he put the last roasting pan into the sink and started to scrub it. Sylvia's shoulders were slumped and he didn't like it. Thirty kids was a lot of responsibility. "The kids are having that English lesson with Pat. I can't believe they'd never heard the Cinderella story until you asked him to read it to them. Anyway, now's a good time to steal a nap. Even Cinderella rested after she scrubbed the fireplace."

"Cinderella never had a kitchen like this to rest in." Sylvia looked around. The midafternoon sun shone through the kitchen window. It was cold enough outside for frost to edge the window, but the hot dishwater made the air moist and warm inside.

She could see Francis's influence in Garth's kitchen. Everything was laid out square, the way a man would do it. But there were touches of red in the geraniums along one counter and in the cozy apple-shaped pot holders along another. These were from Francis.

Sylvia liked Garth's sister and was looking forward to getting to know her better. She might even find out what was making Francis so sad.

"Cinderella doesn't take too long to read. They'll be free in fifteen minutes." Sylvia squared her shoulders. She had more pressing things to do. She needed to start the fairy godmother task. Thankfully she did not have to do the actual work. "And I need to set up a place so you can start to teach them the waltz."

"Me?" Garth stiffened. He'd known this time was coming, but he'd hoped it wouldn't come until he could read the dance book he'd bought in Spokane. He hadn't even diagrammed the steps yet. He wasn't ready. He thought the dancing would come later. Much later. "I—well—I mean it's been a long time since I've waltzed. Since before the army. Did I mention I took a piece of shrapnel in the leg? Don't move as smooth as I used to—I'm sure someone else could teach the kids better."

There. That was only stretching the truth a little, he thought. He had taken a small bit of shrapnel in the leg. And it had been a long, long time since he'd waltzed. Very close to never. And he'd wager his ranch that almost anyone else could teach it better than he could.

Sylvia stopped twisting the tags on the trash bag and set the bag down. She was quiet for a moment, just looking at him. It was going to be harder than she thought to be the fairy godmother. "You don't know how, do you?"

"Well, I—" Garth squirmed. She made it sound so final. "It can't be that hard. I do have a book. I've read a few pages. Doesn't look too hard. Maybe if we put some music on, the kids will just pick it up. They're bright kids. Quick to learn."

"I never learned how to dance much, either," Sylvia said as she sat down on one of the kitchen chairs.

"I left high school too young—went back when I was older." She didn't add that she'd married too young and counted her bruises for those ten years when other kids were out partying. "I seemed to miss all of the dances and…things."

"I only learned the shuffle," Garth admitted as he wiped his hands on the towel he had tied to his belt. He went over and sat down across from Sylvia. "It was enough for what I needed—"

Sylvia arched an eyebrow in question.

Garth grinned. He liked to see the way Sylvia's eyes turned from deep blue to almost turquoise when she was happy or amused. "It gave me an excuse to hold a girl in the dark."

"I don't think that's what Mrs. Buckwalter has in mind." Sylvia smiled. She could almost see a young Garth doing the shuffle in some high school gym draped with purple crepe paper. She'd bet there had been a line of girls ready to snuggle in the dark with him.

"Well, how hard can it be to waltz?" Garth said as he stood up and bowed to Sylvia. "Can I have this dance?"

"Now?"

Garth shrugged. "We've got fifteen minutes to learn. It'd better be now."

Sylvia looked around the kitchen to be sure no one else was there. She wasn't sure why she didn't want to be seen dancing with Garth, but she didn't. "We don't have music."

Garth walked over to a counter and reached up to turn the radio on and then twist the dial. The sounds of a violin trickled into the kitchen. Garth turned the knob higher.

"Not so loud," Sylvia whispered as she looked over her shoulder to the doorway leading into the hall. "We don't want to attract an audience."

Garth felt his breath catch in his throat. Sylvia wanted to dance with him in private. Private was good. Maybe his feelings weren't as far out there as he feared. Maybe she shared some of them, at least.

"It'd destroy their confidence if they knew we don't know, either," Sylvia added.

"Oh."

"First rule of teaching," Sylvia continued. "Give the students confidence in you. First rule of fairy godmothering, too. "

She was blabbering. She knew it. Garth had opened his arms and she had no reason to hesitate about stepping into them. No reason at all except the fear she knew would come when she felt a man touching her. She needed to remind herself that they were only dancing. Exercising really. Aerobics. She could do this. She had to. The kids were counting on her. Mrs. Buckwalter was counting on her. It was like holding her breath under water. She could do it. It wouldn't take long.

"You lead," Sylvia said as she stepped lightly into Garth's arms.

Garth was home. He had his butterfly woman in his arms again and, even if it felt as if she could fly away at any moment, for now she was here and he was home.

"One. Two. The waltz—" Sylvia was breathless.

It must be the counting that calmed her nerves. She was actually feeling less trapped than she'd expected. "Three. The waltz is meant to be danced apart."

Their feet slid across the linoleum. They were in the middle of the floor. Garth led them in a square without bumping into the refrigerator or the table.

"Just like the book says," he noted in surprise. "Block formation. Kind of like football I suppose."

Sylvia stepped farther back from Garth. She had to struggle to hear the sounds of the violin over the thumping of her heart. "One. Two. Three."

Garth didn't care if Sylvia counted to a thousand. He loved to hear the catch in her voice when she talked. Besides, if she didn't count, he'd have to. He had the one diagram in his mind, but even with it, he was having a hard time remembering where they were in the dance.

His attention kept being pulled to the shine of her black hair and the smell of peaches that followed her. And her cheeks—they were lightly pink from the exercise, and he had to remind himself not to reach down and touch them. He didn't want to scare her away. Not now. Not when she was in his arms.

"One. Two." Sylvia made the mistake of looking up and into Garth's eyes. He must be remembering his high school days. His eyes were dark with longing. He was looking at her as if she was all he saw. And it was ridiculous, of course. He must be remembering someone else. The thought didn't comfort her like she thought it would. "Three."

Sylvia tripped.

Garth pulled her closer.

Sylvia would have tripped again if she hadn't been pinned against Garth's chest. She could feel the rhythm of his heart. The buttons on his shirt. The heat of his body. For a moment she wasn't afraid.

Garth held his breath. He could almost hear the emotions chasing themselves up and down Sylvia's spine. He felt the first tremble. That tremble he liked. It was the tremble of a woman in a man's arms when she's suddenly aware of where she is. But it was the second tremble that troubled him. The second tremble was pure fear.

Garth relaxed his hold slowly. He didn't want to startle her further.

"I'd never hurt you," he said simply as he backed even farther away until he was in respectable dance formation again. He looked into her eyes. Their turquoise color had darkened.

Sylvia blushed and looked away. "I know."

The sound of the violins on the radio scratched on and they tried to make the next dance step work, but it didn't. They were out of sync.

"I'm sorry," Sylvia said stiffly. She hated the awkwardness of her problem. That's why she didn't date. Most men expected a woman to be able to tolerate simple things—a hug, an arm around the shoulders, a kiss. A dance. She could do none of those without fear. "It's got nothing to do with you—it's me."

Garth gave up the pretense of dancing. "If it's got to do with you, then it's got to do with me. We can talk about it."

"No point," Sylvia said, moving completely out of Garth's arms. She'd talked about her problems before.

She'd had therapy. She'd made her peace with her past. She'd turned her fear of violence into a positive thing in her work with the kids. It was enough.

Sylvia walked over to the radio. They didn't need the violins anymore.

Garth stood still. He'd known someone was watching them for a bit now. He hadn't heard a sound. He'd sensed breathing—over by the living room door. It was a lifesaving sense he'd developed in the army.

Now the sense was merely inconvenient. Especially out in the barns. He'd get that tingling sensation every time a cow stared at him when his back was turned. He'd assumed the reason for his current prickles was one of the kids, and he hadn't wanted to look because it would break the spell with Sylvia.

"Aren't you even going to kiss her, man?" John's hissed whisper came from the doorway into the living room.

Garth turned around to see four of the teenage boys watching him with disgust on their faces.

"Man, you had her going and you didn't even kiss her!" another one said, more loudly.

Sylvia whirled around. "He did *not* have me going—" She bit her lip. Too much anger would be a tip-off. The boys were bright. "Besides, what are you doing sneaking around? You're supposed to be in class."

"That Cinderella—" one of the boys groaned as they all walked into the kitchen. "The girls are all flapping about it—but it's sissy stuff. There ain't no magic pumpkins. No fairy godmothers, either."

"Well, no, of course, there're no real fairy godmothers,'' Sylvia agreed as she sat down at the kitchen table and gestured for the boys to do the same. ''But that doesn't mean there's not people who help us in life. Like Mrs. Buckwalter—she's helping us.''

John thought a minute and nodded. ''Yeah, she ain't bad.''

''And Garth—he's helping us,'' one of the other boys said as Garth sat down to join them.

''Yes, he is,'' Sylvia forced herself to acknowledge calmly.

''And Mrs. Buckwalter's going on about this thing coming up like it was a royal ball,'' John added. ''Maybe we'll get to see some pumpkin action, after all.''

''Maybe that mean old cow out in the barn—the one with the black ears—maybe she'll turn into a pumpkin,'' one of the boys said, snickering. ''And the chickens can turn into footmen. And some old boot will be a shoe.''

''All I know is we'll have to be home by midnight,'' John grumbled. ''Mrs. Buckwalter already said no one can leave the party alone and go driving around. Don't seem fair when the girls are all going to get new dresses.''

''New dresses!'' Sylvia gasped. They didn't have money for new dresses. Then she remembered. The center wasn't as poor now as it had been last week. Maybe Mrs. Buckwalter was going to write a check. Still, it didn't seem right. Sylvia had no intention of spoiling these kids. They needed to know the value of money. "If the girls are getting new dresses, they'll have to earn them. Chores or something."

Sylvia congratulated herself. Nothing was getting by her. She would help the kids develop character through all of this. It was far too easy for Mrs. Buckwalter to write a check. There needed to be limits.

"Just out of curiosity," Garth began slowly, eyeing each of the teenage boys, "what exactly did you expect to be driving around in?"

Sylvia gulped. She was wrong. Everything was getting by her. She hadn't even heard the slight reference to driving. "And none of you even have driving licenses!"

The boys studied their knuckles.

Finally John cracked. "We weren't planning to go far. Not actually for a drive or anything—"

"Do you realize the penalty for driving without a license?" Sylvia started to lecture. "Especially when you're already on probation! The judges here won't go so easy on you. We don't have Glory to run interference."

"Don't see how anybody would know we'd even done it," John argued. "Ain't no cops around here."

"There might not be any police," Sylvia corrected him firmly, "but believe me, there is a jail and a county sheriff who'd lock you up in a heartbeat."

John, along with the other three boys, went back to studying their knuckles.

"Of course," Garth said thoughtfully. His dark eyes had a twinkle in them. "A man does need to learn how to drive."

"But they're not—" Sylvia bit her tongue. They

might not be men, but they were sensitive. She finished lamely. "They're not of age."

"One of the advantages of being on a farm is that kids can learn to drive earlier if they're driving…say, an old tractor. Out in the field."

Garth should have been a poker player, Sylvia decided. The twinkle in his eyes had hidden deeper until the only clue that he was enjoying himself was a slight smile.

"A tractor?" John looked up in dismay.

"An *old* tractor," Garth continued smoothly. "Goes fifteen miles per hour tops. But she corners good. I learned to drive on her myself. She's nothing fancy, but she moves."

"A tractor?" John asked again. "I was kind of hoping for a pickup."

"Master the tractor this summer," Garth offered, "and we'll talk about the pickup next summer."

Next summer! Sylvia expected the boys to protest that they'd only agreed to come this summer. They never made commitments into the future. She'd have thought they'd declare that next summer they'd be busy with their homeboys. But they didn't.

"Do we get to plough?" Trong, the Vietnamese boy, asked quietly from his corner of the table. "In my home we plough with an ox."

Trong didn't need to add that he missed the earth of his homeland. The longing in his voice said it all.

"The earth is a bit different here," Garth said. "More rock mixed in with it. Nothing like the deep richness of Vietnamese soil. But the smell is close. And when it's freshly turned behind a plough, there's nothing like it. If you want, I'll send you out with one of my hands when the snow clears off the ground. He's going to try tilling some land that we'll be putting into oats this spring. We've had trouble on that bit of land and he thinks a double tilling will do the trick. He'll let you ride with him in the cab."

Sylvia didn't protest that Trong would miss his school lessons. The boy's face lit up with a quiet joy as he eagerly nodded his agreement.

"The rest of you..." Garth looked at the boys sternly. "You can only drive the tractor when I'm around—and only after you've—" Garth had noticed that Sylvia wanted the kids to earn their rewards and he didn't want her to think he was too soft, so he tried to think of something they could do "—only after you've taught the girls to dance."

"Us?" The boys all looked up in startled unison.

"Sure." Garth decided he'd had a stroke of brilliance. "I've seen you guys play basketball. You're light on your feet. Dodging and going in for a setup. You move smooth. All you need is a little coaching and you'll know all the moves."

"Yeah." The boys looked at each other and agreed. "We are pretty good."

"Well, that's settled," Sylvia said as she stood up. She didn't care who taught the kids to dance just as long as she didn't have to spend any more time in Garth's arms. And Garth was right. The boys did have good coordination. "Garth will give you all the pointers you need. We've even cleared a place for you."

Sylvia waved around the kitchen. With the table

moved to the corner, there was room for three or four couples to dance.

"No," Garth said as he stood and addressed the boys. "If we're going to do this, we're going to do it right. There's more room in the barn. We'll assemble the men there."

"Yes, sir!" John said.

Sylvia hid a smile. John was serious. She wondered if the boy even realized how much like a new recruit he sounded or if he was aware of the hero worship that shone on his face. Just because she wasn't always comfortable with Garth, she reminded herself to be thankful for him. He was giving the boys something they lacked—a man to look up to.

Now why had she said that, she thought to herself. She'd had men work with the boys before—kind, gentle men who showed them that a man didn't need to be violent to be worthwhile. But the boys had never bonded with those men like they already had with Garth. And she did not blame them. She'd been so worried about the girls being too attracted to Garth that she hadn't realized it was the boys who shadowed him most.

She wondered briefly if this attachment was good. Garth was, after all, not part of the program. Technically he was their landlord and nothing more. He could break all of their hearts and no one could even fault him. He had a ranch to run. He'd never promised to spend his summer with a bunch of kids.

"Someone else can teach them to dance," Sylvia offered to Garth's back as he and the boys were walking to the door. "I mean, if you have other things to do."

Garth turned and gave her an indignant look as he handed wool jackets to the four boys. "I can teach them."

"I didn't mean you couldn't," Sylvia protested softly. Garth had already pulled his Stetson off a rack by the kitchen door and jammed it on his head. He looked like a man who could do anything.

"Then it's settled." Garth nodded confidently as he opened the door for the boys. "We'll be back when we're done."

Chapter Seven

Sylvia felt the rush of cold air as the door opened and shut behind the boys. It wasn't snowing outside, but the layers from several days ago still covered the ground. She stepped close to the windows and she could see the low mountains in the distance out of the windowpanes. Even the edges of the windows were frosty.

It would be too cold to dance in the barn, she thought to herself, and almost went to the door to call the boys back to give them scarves to wrap around their necks. Then she stopped herself. Maybe suffering while you learned to dance was some kind of male thing. The boys certainly had sense enough to come back inside if they were too uncomfortable.

In the meantime she'd go check on the rest of the kids.

The other boys must have given up on Cinderella, too, because when Sylvia went into the family room where the class had been set up, only the girls were left.

"The closest thing I have to a ball gown is my bathrobe," one of the girls was complaining. Sylvia was surprised. Tara had never shown any inclination to wear any kind of a dress and certainly not something that could be called a gown. "And I sure ain't going to wear that old thing to a dance like the one we're planning."

"I promised we'd go shopping," Mrs. Buckwalter said, her eyes alive with enthusiasm. "I'm sure they have some lovely gowns in—" she looked over at Francis who sat in a nearby chair embroidering on a length of rose satin material "—what is the name of the town again, dear?"

"The closest town is Miles City, but we'd need to go to Billings to get dresses like the ones you're thinking of. There's a little shop, Claire's, that carries a few formals."

"Oh, we'd need more than a few," Mrs. Buckwalter said emphatically. "The girls will all need different dresses."

"Oh." Francis looked up from her sewing and blinked. "Well, I didn't think of that. Claire usually only has three or four styles. The proms aren't until May or so. This time of year she'll only have a few leftover holiday dresses and a basic black or two."

"Well, I'm not wearing my bathrobe," Tara repeated again. "It's all fuzzy."

"Maybe we could sew some simple gowns," Sylvia suggested dubiously. She didn't sew, but Francis made it look easy. "Simple sheaths shouldn't be too hard."

"We don't have time," Francis said as she knotted her thread and set down her sewing. "The reception is Saturday night. We only have two more days and we wouldn't be able to get any fabric until tomorrow. Besides, the girls won't have time for sewing. They'll need to decorate the old barn in town for the wedding dance."

Francis looked at the girls assessingly. "One of them could use my old prom dress if they wanted. Those old dresses are almost in style again."

"I can call my son and have him send us some gowns from Europe. I think he's in Paris this week," Mrs. Buckwalter offered.

"No!" Sylvia jumped into the conversation. Somehow she had a feeling that the less said to Mrs. Buckwalter's son, the better off they all were. He obviously didn't know what his mother was doing yet and Sylvia would like to keep it that way. "There's no need to bother your son. I'm sure—I'm sure there's some other way...."

Sylvia's voice trailed off. She couldn't think of any other way. "Maybe we could glitter up some T-shirts?"

"Absolutely not." Mrs. Buckwalter waved the suggestion aside. "Even Scarlett O'Hara had sense enough to wear her curtains instead of her underwear."

"Madonna wore her slip," one of the girls said brightly. "Maybe we should—"

"Absolutely not!" Mrs. Buckwalter huffed. "This

is a proper dance. I'll not have people in their underwear."

"I have an idea," Francis interrupted quietly. Everyone looked at her. "I think it'll work. I bet half of the women from my graduating class still have a prom dress or two boxed up in their closet. I'm sure they'd be happy to loan them to the girls. That is, if you want them." Francis looked directly at the girls.

"Are those the old fifties dresses?" Tara asked enthusiastically. "Those are so in now."

"Wait a minute, girls. We couldn't possibly ask Francis and her friends to do that," Sylvia protested. "I'm sure those prom dresses are special—they all have memories."

Francis got a faraway look in her eyes and smiled. "Seeing someone else wear the dresses again will only make the memories more real."

"I can pay a rental fee for the dresses," Mrs. Buckwalter offered. "We don't want to be in anyone's debt."

"Don't worry about it," Francis said as she stood up and headed toward the phone. "Send them out for a good dry cleaning and that's all anyone will want. People have talked about the kids coming ever since Garth first called and told us to start getting ready. The people of Dry Creek want to do what they can to help. They're just letting you settle in for a couple of days or they'd already be over with casseroles and homemade bread. Let me call Doris June and Margaret Ann. They'll start the ball rolling for everyone."

"Really? Casseroles?" Sylvia forgot all about the dresses. She supposed it was too much to hope for that the casseroles would be big enough to feed an army.

Sylvia sat down in an overstuffed chair. She could tell the girls were excited because they weren't talking. They were listening to the murmur of Francis's voice on the telephone.

"I wonder if they'll have one with net on it," one of the girls said dreamily. "I've always wanted to dance with net swirling around my legs. Looks so cool in the old movies when the men dip their partners."

"I don't think the boys will be learning about dipping," Sylvia cautioned. She'd never seen so many stars in the eyes of these girls. Usually they showed their tough exterior and, she knew for certain, they were more comfortable in jeans than in lace. Who would have thought that inside they dreamed of being dipped?

After Francis came back and informed the girls that, yes, there would be dance dresses for them, Sylvia wrapped a heavy scarf around her head, put on a ski jacket and walked out to the barn. She knew it was asking too much for the boys to learn to dip, but the happy chatter of the girls made her want to come out and try anyway.

The barn wasn't far from the house, but her breath was coming out in white puffs by the time she arrived there. She didn't have snow boots so she followed in the footsteps the boys had made. The door to the barn was half-open and she stood in the doorway. The light was dim and it took a moment for her eyes to get accustomed.

Straw bales had been pushed back from the main floor of the barn and a couple of milk cows were contentedly corralled off to the side. The main floor had been swept clean—or, Sylvia corrected herself—was being swept clean as she watched.

The teen boys were twirling around the dance floor. Some of them held brooms as partners, with aprons tied around them. Others held shovels. One even held a fence post with a gunny sack tied on top for hair. They were all intently listening as Garth waved his arms like a conductor and called out the best. "One...two...three."

The boys danced stiffly, almost as if they were marching.

"And remember to talk. One...two..." Garth instructed. He was standing in the center of the floor holding a tape recorder with waltz music coming from it. "It's not enough to dance. Three. You need to talk as well."

"Ain't got nothing to say to a broom," one boy said glumly as he stared at his partner and shuffled his feet in formation.

"You ain't got nothing to say to a real girl, either," another shot back.

The other boy stopped dancing and swung his broom back like a club. "Says who?"

Garth moved over to the boys without losing the count. "One...two...three. There'll be no fighting at the dance. Besides, talk isn't hard. You can always tell a girl how pretty she looks. Girls like that."

The boys groaned.

"Or there's the weather," Garth continued as he

punctuated the beat with the toe of his leather boots. "One...two...three. Nice night. Isn't it cold here? One...two...three. That kind of thing. You don't need to be Einstein. Just talk."

The boys obediently began to mumble at their partners.

Sylvia leaned against the doorjamb and watched Garth. His Stetson was pushed back off his forehead and he had a frown of concentration on his face as he counted out the steps. He almost looked as if he thought he could will the boys to dance through his own concentration. Watching him, Sylvia was half-convinced he'd be able to do just that.

"One...two—" Garth looked away from the boys and toward the doorway. His toe stopped tapping and his arms stopped conducting.

Garth blinked. Even with the snow the day was sunny and it took him a moment to realize that Sylvia was standing in the doorway. She had her hair wrapped up in a soft white knit scarf that was tucked under her chin. The sun streamed in behind her and gave her a halo. She looked adorable.

Garth realized he'd stopped counting when he no longer heard the brush of the brooms on the barn floor. The boys had stopped dancing and were looking at him in confusion.

"Three," Garth resumed. "One—"

The brushing resumed.

"Miss Sylvia, look at us," one of the boys called out as he moved with his broom. "We're dancing."

"I see," Sylvia agreed. "And you're doing fine."

"Dance with us," another boy invited. "Mr. Elkton has an extra shovel."

"Two—" Garth kept his mind focused. He didn't tell the boys, but in his opinion this was the problem with dancing. Being close to a woman made it difficult for a man to concentrate. And, if nothing else, dancing required concentration. "Three."

"One." Garth stopped even trying. Sylvia had taken the shovel and was twirling it around and laughing with the boys.

Another figure appeared in the doorway.

"Garth?" It was Francis. She'd thrown a coat over her shoulders and come out without a scarf. "Phone call for you."

"I'll call them back later."

"It's a strange call," Francis said quietly, walking closer to Garth until she could talk without the boys hearing her. "Some man insists he needs to talk to you right now but he won't tell me who he is or what it's about—just said you need to come."

"Probably just a salesman," Garth said, keeping his voice calm. He didn't want everyone upset. "You know how persistent they can be."

"We don't get many sales calls out here."

"Maybe it's someone from that new feed supplement company I'm trying. I sent in a form for more information." Garth set the tape recorder down on a straw bale and pulled his Stetson down farther before he started to walk toward the barn door.

Before he stepped outside, Garth turned and called, "Keep dancing. I'll expect you to be pros by the time I get back."

Some of the boys grunted. Others just bit their lips in concentration and began to count to their dance partners.

"Want a shovel?" Sylvia stopped twirling and offered her shovel to Francis. "It's kind of fun."

Francis pulled her wool coat more closely around her shoulders. Her face was pale and strained. She was clearly worried.

"It's probably just a salesman, like Garth said." Sylvia laid down the shovel and quietly walked over and put her arm around the other woman's shoulders.

Francis nodded slowly. "It's just that the voice was so intense…and it sounded like—like someone I used to know."

"Well, maybe that's it. Maybe it is someone you know and they just want to talk to Garth about something."

"No." Francis shook her head. "This man would never call here. I used to think so. But, no, he'd never call. Not after all those years. It's just that it made me remember—" Francis pulled her coat tighter around herself and smiled. "But enough of that. Old memories are just that. Old."

"Is there anything I can do to help?" Sylvia asked. Francis's smile didn't reach her eyes. Her lips moved, but it was clear the smile meant little. "I'm a pretty good listener."

"I wish there was something somebody could do," Francis said, her voice low and intense. "I thought by coming back here I could lay my ghosts to rest, but it hasn't worked that way—every place I look, I remember him."

"Ahh," Sylvia said sympathetically. "Old boyfriend?"

Francis tried to smile again. This time her lips only twisted. "We were married. Briefly. Or so I thought."

"Oh, I didn't know you'd been married."

"We weren't. The ceremony was fake," Francis said bitterly. "Turned out he wasn't the staying-around kind. Never even bothered to leave a note. Just left. Garth was in the army so he didn't even know about it. By the time he came back, there was no point in telling him."

"It must have been lonely."

"It was better when I moved to Denver. But I could never completely shake the memories so I decided to come back and face them. I thought they'd go away here."

Sylvia hugged her. "It's always best to face our past. Believe me, I know."

"You?" Francis looked up in surprise. "You look like you have it all together."

Sylvia laughed as the two of them started toward the barn door. "Believe me, I could tell you stories."

After walking back to the house in the crusted snow, Sylvia thought the inside of the kitchen felt stuffy warm. She slipped her tennis shoes off and sat down on a bench by the door. The thick wool socks she wore were wet and she pulled them off. She unwrapped her scarf and then stood to hang up her jacket. The kitchen floor was cold and her feet were still tingling as she started to walk farther into the house.

By then Francis was standing beside the kitchen

counter. "I'm going to make us a cup of tea and we'll talk."

"Sounds good to me. I'm just going to go borrow some socks from one of the girls. I think they brought a few extra pairs over to the house this morning."

Sylvia could hear Garth's murmured phone conversation when she stepped into the hallway that connected the kitchen to both the living room and Garth's den. She couldn't hear the words, but his low tone coming from the den sounded cautious and reserved.

"Anyone have extra socks?" Sylvia asked as she stepped into the living room. The girls were sitting at the long table, doing what looked like homework. When she got closer, she saw they had spread out old dress patterns.

"We're learning about multiplication," Mrs. Buckwalter explained. "We're taking a twenty-five-inch-waist pattern and altering it to fit someone with a twenty-eight-inch waist. Then we're going to learn about doing some simple sewing—hems and turning up cuffs."

"I always have trouble with jeans being too long," one of the shorter girls explained.

Sylvia had never realized the girls might want to learn these kind of homemaking skills. "I don't suppose anyone is dying to learn how to cook?" she asked hopefully.

"I can flip burgers," one girl said proudly.

"And eggs," another added.

"Want to help with breakfast tomorrow?"

The two girls shrugged. "Sure."

"Good. They can help with the lobsters, too," Mrs. Buckwalter looked up from the dress patterns and said matter-of-factly. "We'll need some cooks for that—"

"I've never cooked lobsters," one of the girls said hesitantly.

"Don't worry." Mrs. Buckwalter dismissed the concerns with a wave of her hand. "I've watched my chef do it, and it's easier than cooking burgers. Anyone who can boil up a big pot of hot water can cook a lobster."

"Oh." The girl brightened. "I can do that. Boiling water."

"Surely there's more to it than that," Sylvia said dubiously. "I mean I've never cooked one myself, but it just seems there'd be more to it."

"Sometimes things are easier than we think," Mrs. Buckwalter said airily. "I think our big challenge will be getting pots big enough for all the water. That, and finding a store in Miles City that will deliver live lobster."

"Have you asked Francis about stores yet?" Sylvia almost fell to her knees. They were saved. Why didn't she think of that? There was no way a store in Miles City would have a hundred live lobsters just waiting around for a dinner party. They'd have to settle for finger sandwiches, after all. "There might not be any lobsters available."

"Well, surely no one else has bought them all," Mrs. Buckwalter stated blankly. "It's not Christmas."

"I'm not sure they routinely stock lobsters in the stores here," Sylvia said gently. "We're a long way from the coast and it's in the middle of cattle country."

"Why, I guess we are." Mrs. Buckwalter sounded surprised as she thought about it. "I'm just so used to Seattle. Don't know what I was thinking. But, of course, we're in cattle country. I've heard Garth mumble about those cattle rustlers ever since we got here."

"You have? I haven't heard him say a word about them. I thought they might not strike again."

"Oh, they're here all right," Mrs. Buckwalter said complacently. "That's another reason Garth didn't want the boys off driving by themselves. Don't know who they'll meet up with in these hills."

"That does it," Sylvia said as she took an extra pair of socks offered by one of the teenagers. "I'm sleeping with the girls in their bunkhouse again tonight instead of in the guest room here. I never thought about the rustlers still being active."

"Oh, they wouldn't come this close to the house," Mrs. Buckwalter assured her with a wink and a raised eyebrow, showing she knew all the girls were listening intently to her words. "I'm sure if everyone's tucked into bed by...say ten o'clock, we've got nothing to worry about."

"Ten o'clock," one of the girls wailed. "That's barely even nighttime."

"Well, we all need our beauty rest anyway," Mrs. Buckwalter continued as she turned back to the dress patterns. "I asked Francis to call the hairdresser in town and she's coming out tomorrow for anyone who wants to have their hair done for the dance."

"I hope she can do a fifties look," another girl said as she shook her long hair. "If we have the dresses, I want to look the part. Maybe one of those braids."

"I'm sure she can do whatever you want with your hair," Mrs. Buckwalter said firmly.

Sylvia sat down in a chair and pulled the socks on her feet. "I can't wait to see everyone all dressed up."

"Bet we look better than the boys," one of the girls bragged.

"We better," another girl muttered. "It'll take us all day to get ready."

Sylvia started to walk to the kitchen in her warm socks. The socks were a little big, but cozy. Just the thing to wear when drinking a cup of tea with Francis and talking.

The wood floor in the hallway was slick and Sylvia slid in her socks. The door to the den was open and she could hear Garth's phone conversation. She realized he didn't know anyone was there because he heard no footsteps. She cleared her throat. She didn't want to eavesdrop even unintentionally. She heard Garth put down the receiver and mutter to himself. By the time she reached the door of the den he was coming out of the room.

"Oh, I didn't know anyone was there," Garth said as he ran his hands through his hair. Even with his tan, his face was pale and he had a frown on his forehead. "I don't suppose you heard the conversation?"

"Me? No. I just came into the hallway."

"Too bad. I could use a second opinion." Garth

said, running his hands through his hair again. "Some crackpot who won't say his name calls up. Just tells me to watch Francis and not let her out of the house alone. I try to talk to him, but he won't say any more. Said the phones could be tapped."

"Did he sound rational?" Sylvia drew in her breath. She knew the drill. She was betting Francis did recognize that voice. Sylvia had seen enough violent confrontations between spouses to know that nothing was surprising—not even a boyfriend who waited twenty years to exact his revenge. "Did he sound like he was drinking or on drugs? Did he make any specific threat? Did he mention a knife or a gun?"

"Why no—" Garth sounded surprised. He looked at Sylvia. "Why would he? He can't even know Francis if he would want to hurt her. Francis makes friends with everyone. I don't think she has an enemy in the world."

Sylvia watched her words. She didn't want to betray Francis's confidence. "Maybe you should ask her. She might know of someone."

"I think we should do that," Garth said with authority as he started toward the kitchen. "Nobody's going to threaten my sister and get away with it."

Francis was just setting two mugs filled with hot tea on the table when Garth walked into the kitchen, followed by Sylvia.

"We need to talk," Garth said as he pulled out a chair and gestured for Sylvia to sit down at the table.

"Well, let me make you a cup of coffee, then. I

know you don't like tea," Francis said as she turned her back to walk to the cupboard.

"I don't need anything," Garth said as he pulled out another chair for Francis. "Sit down and talk with us."

"But you should have something hot. It's cold out and you never take a break." Francis turned and fussed at him but didn't sit down. "It'll only take a minute to make a pot of coffee. You need to take care of yourself. It won't hurt you to relax."

"Today all I've done is relax," Garth protested. "And you know I can get my own coffee if I want it. Nobody needs to wait on me."

"But it's the least I can do—and you never take time in the middle of the day to just sit and talk," Francis said as she walked back to the table and sat down. "I think it's a good sign. You're not so worried about everything with the rustlers and all."

Garth realized with a start that he hadn't thought about the rustlers all day. He'd gotten so involved with the kids and then this call about Francis. Getting that call reminded him that there were things in his life much more valuable to him than his cattle. He'd rather lose all his cattle than have someone hurt Francis.

"Rustlers aren't the only bad people in the world," Garth said slowly. He didn't just want to spring his question on Francis. But how did one ask it? "I don't suppose you've known many bad people."

"Bad people?" Francis asked blankly.

"You know, someone who threatened to hurt you. Or said they wanted something bad to happen to you?'' Garth worked his way through the questions as best as he could.

''Me?''

Garth finally looked at Sylvia in appeal.

''He means someone who might hurt you,'' Sylvia said softly.

Francis looked at both of them in bewilderment. ''Why would anyone hurt me?''

''Sometimes,'' Sylvia spoke carefully, ''people who love us—or who say they love us—can decide to hurt us.''

''But who—'' Francis started, and then seemed to realize what Sylvia was implying. ''Oh, no, he would never hurt me.''

''He?'' Garth asked.

Francis looked at Sylvia and then back at Garth. ''My almost husband.''

Surprise rocked Garth back in his chair. ''Husband! When were you married?''

''Almost. When I was eighteen,'' Francis answered calmly.

''But,'' Garth sputtered, ''you never said—''

''You were over in Asia,'' Francis said with a soft smile. ''It all happened so fast. Dad had hired him to help with the branding that summer. He fired Flint quick enough when he realized Flint had asked me to the prom and then took me to Vegas, but it was too late.''

''You could have written.'' Garth persisted. ''I did get mail.''

Francis smiled an apology to her brother. ''Flint left me after we got back from Vegas. The ceremony was fake. I haven't heard from him since. I didn't want you to know—I didn't want anyone to know. I was ashamed to be such a fool.''

"Oh, no," Sylvia murmured as she put her hand over Francis's. "You were no fool. He was the fool to leave a woman like you."

Francis smiled wryly. "I like to think that's true. In any event, I haven't heard from him since, so you see it's not possible that he's thinking of harming me. I'm sure he hasn't even thought of me for years.''

"But you said he reminded you of the voice on the telephone," Sylvia pressed. "Do you think it could have been him?"

Francis's face drained of color and her fingers gripped the handle of her mug filled with tea. "No, it's not possible.''

Sylvia looked at Garth and saw her thoughts reflected in his eyes. Francis was wrong. It could be Flint.

"Just to be safe," Sylvia said casually, "you might stay by the house. No trips alone to Miles City or anything.''

"I haven't planned to go anywhere," Francis said. She was still gripping the handle of her mug, but the color was returning to her face. "Oh, except with the kids tomorrow to help decorate the barn. We're stringing crepe paper banners. It's becoming quite a production. But then, I always love wedding receptions.'' Francis looked down at her fingers. "Never had one of my own. The closest I got to it was the prom. Flint took me and we—'' Francis looked up and said briskly, "Well, enough of that. We went and had a good time. But it's over. And I can guarantee he's not waiting around to get his revenge for my bad dancing. That's all in the past. Goodness, it's been twenty years.''

Francis pushed back her chair and stood up. ''Besides, he has no reason to be angry with me. None at all.''

''It doesn't always take a reason,'' Sylvia said quietly as she, too, cupped the warmth of her tea mug.

''Did the man on the phone actually threaten me?'' Francis turned to Garth and asked.

''Well, no,'' Garth said reluctantly. ''He said he was calling to warn me that someone else might try to kidnap or hurt my sister.''

''Well, see then,'' Francis said decisively. ''He wasn't threatening me at all. He was just worried.''

''It doesn't always work that way,'' Sylvia offered. ''Quite often men who are abusive in relationships don't think they mean to harm the person. They don't accept the responsibility for their actions. They always think the threat is someone else even if it's only another side of themselves.''

''Well, it can't be Flint. It just can't be.'' Francis walked to the refrigerator and opened the door. ''I say we just forget about it and have some chocolate cake with our tea.''

Garth watched Sylvia as she moved her mug closer to herself. She wrapped her fingers around it like it was a heater. It wasn't cold in the house. If anything, it was too warm. But Sylvia looked like she was shivering.

''There's nothing to be afraid of,'' Garth said hesitantly while Francis took the cake out of the refrigerator. He wasn't sure it was physical fear that was making Sylvia tremble, but he offered her what he could. "I wouldn't let anything happen to anyone. And there's eight cowboys roaming around the place all day long. Believe me, if there's someone here who doesn't belong, they'll find him."

"I know." Sylvia looked up and smiled at Garth. "It's just reflex action. Too many memories."

"You can tell me about them."

"Sometime. Maybe." Sylvia wondered if she ever could. She'd only talked about the abuse in her marriage with her minister and with her therapist. She didn't usually discuss it. She'd told a few friends when it first happened, but she gradually realized that they'd begun looking at her as though she had done something to prompt the violence. She felt like telling them she wished she had caused it. Then she'd know how to make it stop.

"If someone's hurt you, I'll—" Garth began and stopped when he saw the startled look on Sylvia's face. He could tell she wasn't ready for the intensity of his protective emotion toward her.

"You'll do nothing," Sylvia said flatly. "I can't abide violence."

"It's not violence to protect someone you—" Garth stopped himself and stumbled over the words. "Someone who's—who's living in your house."

Sylvia started breathing again. For a moment she'd thought Garth was going to say "someone you love." But that was silly. He barely knew her. He was just the kind of man who would protect a stray cat if it was on his property.

"Okay, who wants cake?" Francis asked as she set some plates on the table.

"I'll have half a piece," Sylvia said. It was clear Francis was choosing to ignore the warning from the phone call. And maybe she was right. Sylvia wondered if she'd been around violence for so long in her life that she expected it even when it wasn't coming.

"I should get back to the boys," Garth exclaimed as though he'd just remembered them. "I have them out there twirling around to an old tape of Lawrence Welk and practicing their conversation."

"Do you think they could learn dipping while they're at it?" Sylvia asked. "The girls would like that."

"Dipping?" Garth shook his head incredulously as he stood up and walked toward the door. "I'm not sure I can teach them to keep time to the music—let alone dipping! I don't even know if that's diagrammed in my book!"

"You'll find a way," Francis said serenely. "And when you do, it'll be perfect."

Garth grunted as he pulled on his coat and walked out the door.

Francis smiled mischievously when Garth closed the door. "He hates it when I tease him about being perfect. But I tell him that's what sisters do. Besides, he usually does manage to pull it off—whatever he sets his mind to—"

"Well, it would be nice if he could teach them to

dip,'' Sylvia said as she took a sip of the tea in her mug. Raspberry-flavored. "Mmm, good."

"But it's probably cold by now. We were talking so long." Francis fussed as she stood. "Let me get you another cup."

"No, this is just right," Sylvia protested, and waved Francis back to her seat. "Besides, I want you to tell me all about this secret boyfriend of yours."

Francis's face lit up and Sylvia's heart sank. Sylvia hoped she was wrong about that phone call because it was clear that Francis still was starry-eyed and in love with her Flint.

Meanwhile, at the Billings airport

Flint gripped the receiver of the pay phone. He knew he'd been foolish to call and warn Garth Elkton. He'd tried to talk himself out of it all during the plane trip from Seattle. There were many reasons why he shouldn't call. He knew them all. The phone could be tapped. Even if the phone wasn't tapped, someone could be planted as a spy within the Elkton household and Garth would undoubtedly talk even if Flint told him not to.

And then there was the fact that Flint couldn't explain who he was. He knew Garth would wonder why a special agent was being assigned to the case when nothing had happened. People receive idle threats all the time. Special agents don't come to check them out. The truth was Garth wouldn't believe Flint was on his side no matter what he said on the telephone.

But even knowing all the reasons, Flint had headed for the pay phone the minute he'd walked off the plane. Even if nobody listened, he'd had to warn Garth that someone was going to kidnap Francis.

Chapter Eight

The early-morning chill made the walk from the bunkhouse to the main house a quick one for Sylvia. The gray morning light promised an overcast day and the snow-crusted ground still looked trampled from yesterday. Heavy clouds gathered around the Big Sheep Mountains and Sylvia rubbed her hands together to keep them warm. She could see her own breath—puffs of white that warmed her hands when she cupped them around her nose.

She hadn't looked in the mirror before she left the bunkhouse. She knew what she would see. She'd scrubbed her face with lukewarm water and twisted her hair up into a casual bun. The outside cold would have made her face tight and fragile looking. This weather was not kind to someone over forty.

But Sylvia wasn't in any beauty contest. She wore a man's flannel shirt with the sleeves rolled up and well-worn denim jeans with no designer labels in sight. They were the warmest clothes she'd brought with her, and she still buttoned the jacket Francis had loaned her all the way up to her chin. She must look a sight. Not that it mattered. She had more important things to worry about than beauty.

Still, when she started up the steps of the kitchen porch, she wondered if she shouldn't have turned a light on earlier in the bunkhouse so she could at least run a lipstick over her mouth. But turning on a light would have awakened the girls sleeping in their cots and she had decided they needed to rest.

The girls had fallen asleep late last night even though Sylvia had insisted they turn the lights out at eleven. Sylvia was amazed at how excited the girls were about the dance.

But then, Sylvia said to herself as she topped the stairs, she was getting excited herself. She could hardly wait to see the girls in their dresses. This dance was turning her kids into normal, not-a-care-in-the-world teenagers. Maybe Mrs. Buckwalter was right. A dress-up event did seem to bring out the best in everyone.

Sylvia twisted the kitchen door knob before she remembered Garth had locked all the doors and windows last night.

"Who's there?" someone called out softly, startling Sylvia until she recognized Garth's voice.

Sylvia looked again. The kitchen windows were covered with thick frost, but they were all dark.

"It's me, Sylvia."

The kitchen door swung open. The room was dark except for the illuminated hands on the clock above the stove. It was five-thirty. The smells of last night's hamburgers still lingered. The kitchen looked like it had before Sylvia left last night. Garth had washed the skillets and set them to dry by the sink. The table in the middle of the room had two big round boxes of oatmeal sitting in its center. She and Garth had announced at dinner that it would be oatmeal for breakfast. The teens had groaned until Garth had promised to put raisins and cinnamon in it.

And then Sylvia saw what was different in the kitchen. Garth had obviously pulled an armchair out of the living room and into the far corner of the room last night after everyone had left. A pillow and a rumpled blanket showed he had slept there. A sturdy baseball bat lay on the floor along with the telephone.

"You are worried, aren't you?" Sylvia shivered. She'd almost convinced herself that Francis was right and that the phone call was nothing more than a wrong number.

Garth stood and nodded. He rubbed one hand over his head. His chestnut hair was tousled and reminded Sylvia of the rich grains of a fine piece of mahogany. "The man on the phone just sounded so sure of himself. He didn't sound like a drunk at all."

"Is there someplace you could send Francis? Someplace away from here?"

Garth grunted. "Ever try talking sense to Francis? She wouldn't go. She doesn't look it, but she's one stubborn woman."

"Takes after her big brother, I bet." Sylvia smiled.

Garth had a shadow of dark whiskers across his face and his hair needed combing. He had on an old sweatshirt with a tear in the sleeve and he was wearing slippers instead of shoes, but Sylvia swore he looked every inch a knight in white armor. Francis was lucky to have an older brother like him.

"Maybe I am overly cautious," Garth said. "Stayed up all night and all I heard was the howl of the wind. Besides, I'd hear a car or truck before it came close. Not much chance someone could sneak up on us that way. A car engine has to work to make it up that rise."

"And you know nobody's going to walk in this far from the main road," Sylvia agreed as she took off the jacket she'd borrowed from Francis last night. The kitchen was warmer than outside, but not much warmer. "I'll set the water to boiling. I don't know how big of a pot we'll need for all that oatmeal."

Sylvia turned as she hung the jacket up on a hook and walked toward the table. "You'll have to show me where the raisins are."

"Hmph," Garth grunted.

Now what was wrong with him, Sylvia thought to herself as she looked over at his scowl. "If you don't have raisins, we can use dried dates or just make do with the cinnamon."

"We've got raisins," Garth said curtly.

"Well, then—" Sylvia prompted.

"Plenty of raisins." Garth walked back to his chair. "Use as many as you want. Raisins are good for the kids."

"Well, yes, all right, if you're sure." Sylvia walked over to the table and picked up a large box of oatmeal. If he wasn't going to say what was bothering him, she wasn't going to dig it out of him.

"Nice shirt," Garth said, his back turned as he folded the blanket he'd used while sleeping in the chair. "Belong to a friend?"

"You like it? You can order one from the catalog if you want. I buy men's shirts sometimes for when I do repairs around the center. They're roomier in the shoulders so I can move better."

"So there's no friend."

Sylvia paused, oatmeal box in midair. Oh, no, it's that time, Sylvia moaned to herself. She needed to pull out her speech about why she didn't date. She was collecting her words when Garth turned around.

"No, I don't suppose there's one," Garth said cheerfully.

It took a moment for Garth's words to sink in.

"What? Why not?" Even though Sylvia was ready to tell Garth that she didn't date, it was altogether different for him to assume she wouldn't have a boyfriend. She could have a boyfriend if she wanted. That was altogether different than choosing not to date.

"Well, if you were dating anyone," Garth said, "I would know by now. Those kids can't keep a secret."

"They can keep a secret if they don't know a secret," Sylvia said airily as she turned to the cupboard and opened the door to the shelves that held the pots and pans. Let him chew on that. She pulled out a soup pot. "I don't necessarily tell everyone about my personal life."

"Oh."

"Now where do you keep the cinnamon?" Sylvia

asked as she turned on the faucet to fill the pot with water. "I suppose we wait until the oatmeal is done before we add the cinnamon, but I'd like to get it ready."

"We need to make toast, too," Garth offered sourly. "And I'll put on a fresh pot of coffee." He turned to her. "Would you really keep a secret from those kids?"

Sylvia smiled at him. "Would you keep a secret from Francis?"

"Not the kind she keeps from me." Garth grunted and then looked at her fiercely. "I hope you're not going to tell me you have some husband hanging around, too, that you've conveniently forgotten to mention."

Sylvia chuckled. Even though she definitely wasn't interested in dating, it was nice to know someone cared whether or not she did. "No. No husband. Not anymore."

"Hmph. Well, that's good, anyway."

The oatmeal was lumpy. Sylvia didn't know why. She'd stirred oatmeal before and it had never turned lumpy on her like this. Of course, she admitted, she'd never made a six-quart pot of oatmeal before. She had hoped the kids would think the lumps were just extra raisins. It hadn't worked.

"They want more toast." Francis limped into the kitchen carrying an empty tray. It was her fifth trip in the past ten minutes. "And the jelly's running out."

"We don't have any more jelly," Mrs. Buckwalter said, bending down to the check the lower shelf in the cupboard. "We have jellied cranberry sauce—and pickle relish."

"We'll use the cranberry sauce," Garth said as he flipped the slices of bread he was grilling in the oven's broiler. He had given up on the toaster several platters earlier. "They might not notice the difference. It's red and they'll be able to spread it."

"I thought we bought a big jar of that grape jelly last week." Francis turned to Garth.

"Gone. The boys needed a snack yesterday after their dance lessons."

"Thank God we need to go to Dry Creek this afternoon to see about decorations for the reception," Mrs. Buckwalter said as she lifted two cans of cranberry sauce off the shelf.

"They'll still be hungry whether they're in Dry Creek or here," Francis said.

"But we can buy them lunch at that café I hear about," Mrs. Buckwalter said emphatically.

"But that'll be expensive," Francis worried. "They do tend to eat rather a lot. Linda's prices aren't high, but it would take a lot of food."

"I'd rather spend the money," Mrs. Buckwalter said as she picked up a can opener and sat down at the kitchen table. She twisted the handle of the opener around the first can of cranberry sauce. "My accountant will understand."

"You have a project accountant?" Sylvia laid out more bread slices to grill.

"More or less," Mrs. Buckwalter said grimly. "My son promoted him to Chief Financial Officer—

now all the bills funnel through Robert himself. Remember my son?''

Sylvia dropped a slice of bread and then nodded. Of course, she remembered the woman's son, Robert. The one who was in Europe. The one who wanted to give all the foundation's money to museums. He was the last person she wanted to see their bills. Especially not a bill for thirty orders of hamburgers and fries from a small café in Dry Creek.

''Maybe we should try tuna sandwiches,'' Sylvia suggested brightly. She looked a little dubiously at the empty plastic wrappers that had come off the loaves of bread Garth had toasted. She wondered if there would be enough bread left for sandwiches. But they could make them open-faced if necessary. ''That way we won't bother Robert.''

''Oh, we won't bother him anyway.'' Mrs. Buckwalter fussed as she scooped the cranberry sauce out of the can and into several small bowls. ''The bills will just sit on his desk until his secretary decides they need to be paid and sends them down to Accounting. Especially when he's in Europe. All he gets are printouts. By e-mail at that. I've told him he needs to take more of an interest in the actual bills, but you know how boys are—they never listen to their mothers.''

''Well, hamburgers it is, then,'' Sylvia said in relief. Garth had just removed the last bread crust from the last plastic bag and slipped it onto the broiler pan. They would have had to use crackers anyway.

''I'll call Linda and let her know we're coming,'' Francis offered as she started to walk toward the telephone. "We can't just spring this one on her—I don't know what she keeps around for supplies."

"You're going, too?" Garth asked Francis.

Francis turned around just before entering the hallway. "Of course."

"Then tell her to figure on enough to feed me and the hands, too. I'm not taking any chances on that phone call. The farm chores can wait—besides, everyone enjoys a day in town now and again. Even Jess," Garth said.

"If Linda needs to go into Miles City for supplies, ask her if she can find a place to order the lobsters," Mrs. Buckwalter called out as she pulled another can of jellied cranberry sauce from the bottom cupboard.

"I don't think there will be any lobsters in Miles City, either," Francis said from the hallway. "But I'll ask. Maybe there's some kind of frozen ones."

"Frozen?" Mrs. Buckwalter stood up straight, a horrified expression on her face. "Oh, no, that would never do."

Sylvia exchanged a quick glance with Garth and then looked at the older woman and offered softly, "No one expects more than maybe a sandwich and some potato salad. It's just being together as a community and celebrating the wedding that is the fun part."

"No," Mrs. Buckwalter squared her shoulders and said firmly. "I've said I'll give everyone lobsters and lobsters it will be. A Buckwalter does not go back on her word."

The café in Dry Creek had changed since Sylvia was there at Christmastime. Of course, the Christmas garlands had been taken down and all that remained of the hitman who had been hunting Glory Beckett was a picture on the cork bulletin board of him posing as Santa Claus.

Sylvia murmured a prayer of thanks remembering how close her friend Glory had come to being killed. They had all thought the boys were lying when they claimed another hit man had been sent. As it turned out, the boys had been going to Dry Creek to try and protect Glory instead of to kill her.

Sylvia glanced sideways at Garth. He had quickly looked inside the restaurant before stepping back to open the screen door for everyone. Sylvia could tell he was trying to be casual, but she saw him look over at that photo on the bulletin board, too. They had all miscalculated before and not listened to the boys' warning—*Please, Lord, don't let it happen again. Help us heed the warning and watch out for Francis. Keep her safe.*

"Oh, I love what you've done," Francis softly exclaimed as she entered the café and looked around.

Linda was walking toward the door and tying on a large white apron. Her long brown hair was pulled back into a ponytail and two hoop earrings hung from each ear. She beamed back at Francis. "Thank you."

"It *is* nice," Sylvia agreed.

The floor had been re-covered in checkered black and white tiles. The tables were topped with gray Formica, and each held an old-fashioned pair of glass salt and pepper shakers. Healthy geranium plants hung from several hooks in the ceiling, red blossoms peeking out from beneath abundant green leaves. White café curtains covered the bottom half of the windows. The photos on the bulletin board showed several birthday parties that had obviously been held at the café.

"Sort of a fifties diner look," Sylvia noted.

"You can tell?" Linda asked eagerly. "That's what we wanted it to look like, but we weren't sure. We wanted to order some stuff from a catalog but we couldn't afford it yet so we had to work with what we had. We laid the tile ourselves and my brothers helped us resurface the tables."

"It's lovely," Mrs. Buckwalter said emphatically, entering the diner behind the last of the kids. "You can tell it's the kind of place that takes the comfort of its customers seriously."

"Looks like the kind of place that has malted shakes," John said hopefully as he and several of the other kids arranged themselves around one of the tables. "The kind with real ice cream."

"That stuff'll kill you," K.J. said mournfully.

"Not today it won't," John retorted briefly while eyeing Linda. "You do have them, don't you?"

Linda nodded. "Any kind of shake you want—strawberry, chocolate, vanilla or mint—and bacon cheeseburgers with ranch fries, or chili dogs and onion rings..."

"Goodness, I couldn't have any of that." The older woman shook her head. "K.J. reminded me. My chef would scold me for sure if I even thought about it."

"You have a chef?" Jess, his hat pushed back, asked indignantly. "And you're going on about my diet. Anybody can watch their diet when they're spoon-fed by some sissy Frenchman.''

"It's not some sissy Frenchman," Mrs. Buckwalter said complacently. "Jenny is Irish. Cute young thing. My son gave her to me for Christmas. He's worried about my health so I had to promise to eat right when I left Jenny in Seattle. She would have insisted on coming with me if I hadn't said I'd stick to my diet." Mrs. Buckwalter looked at Jess and added self-righteously, "Besides, it won't hurt either one of us to eat healthy. At our age."

Jess gave an indignant snort.

"Wait a minute." Sylvia hoped she was hearing right. "Your chef could have come with you? Here—to Dry Creek?"

"Well, it's a good thing she didn't," Mrs. Buckwalter said. "Then she wouldn't have been in Seattle to take my call and have all those lobsters shipped to us."

Sylvia's heart sank. "You asked her to ship us lobsters?"

"Of course. There are no lobsters here. Francis even called into Billings for me. Not a lobster in sight. But they can be ordered. Jenny can order anything in the world."

"I don't suppose she could order the lobsters to be cooked and then shipped."

"Of course not. Everyone knows lobsters have to be alive when they're cooked. We can worry about it after lunch." Mrs. Buckwalter turned to Linda. "Now, dear, what else do you have besides hamburgers?"

"We also have grilled turkey burgers—or veggie burgers—and a side of fresh vegetables," Linda continued proudly. "Mostly carrots and green pepper slices this time of year with a little bit of jicama."

"Perfect," Mrs. Buckwalter said as she lowered herself into a seat at one of the kids' tables. "Jess and I will have the veggie burgers with vegetables."

Jess grunted. "Make mine a double ch—" Mrs. Buckwalter frowned at him and he finished lamely, "A double on the vegetables. Extra green pepper if you have it."

The boys and Garth's ranch hands were having pie at the café still when Linda got a telephone call saying several women were delivering prom dresses to the hardware store.

"They have that big rack in back where Matthew hangs the horse bridles. It's high enough up so none of the hems will touch the floor," Linda reported as she slid the last pieces of pie into place on the table where the ranch hands were sitting. She looked at Jess. His was the only place at the ranch hands' table that didn't have a piece of apple pie at it. "I've got some extra apples in back. I could slice you some fruit and put a sprinkle of cinnamon on it. It'd be almost like pie."

"No, thanks," Jess said mournfully. "It wouldn't be the same."

"Your arteries will thank you," Mrs. Buckwalter encouraged from across the room.

Jess grunted. "They better 'cause my stomach sure won't."

"Here, have a toothpick." One of the other hands held up a small jar of wrapped toothpicks. "That is—" the man looked over at Mrs. Buckwalter and grinned "—if it's allowed on your new diet."

"Mark my words, young man." Mrs. Buckwalter stood and walked toward Jess's table. "You'll be better off eating toothpicks than double cheeseburgers with fries."

"Who can think about food? How many of the dresses are here?" one of the girls asked eagerly as she started to rise from her table. "And where is the hardware store?"

"I'll show you," Francis said as she stood.

When Garth and the ranch hands stood, too, Francis glanced over at her brother. "Really, Garth, there's no need. We're in Dry Creek. I'm perfectly safe here. When was the last time a stranger even came to Dry Creek?"

Francis's indignant question hung in the air for a few moments before she realized what she had said, and then sat down. "But that was different. The hit man was after Glory Beckett because she'd seen that crime committed and she knew something. I've never seen a crime committed. I don't know any dangerous secrets. No one has any reason to put a contract out on me."

"Of course not," Sylvia agreed easily. "But you know what they say about an ounce of prevention—"

"I suppose you're right," Francis said as she folded her hands.

Sylvia hadn't noticed the kids looking at each other until one of the girls asked, "Is something wrong?"

"There's nothing to worry about," Sylvia said firmly. She didn't want the kids to have to worry about anything when they seemed so happy these days.

"Sylvia's right," Garth said, and then he looked at Sylvia. "There is no need to worry. But it is good for you to know that we got a threatening phone call yesterday. We're just making sure everyone stays safe."

"Was it a gang?" John asked indignantly.

"Oh, surely not." Sylvia was startled. She hadn't even thought of the rival gang. "They're back in Seattle. They wouldn't—" She looked over at Garth. Could they?

"It was only a telephone call," Garth said thoughtfully. "Now that you mention it, it didn't sound local. Lots of noise in the background, like it was coming from a pay phone. But how would they know about Francis?"

"Did the man on the phone actually say my name?" Francis asked.

"Well, no, I think he said 'your sister.' But how would some kids in Seattle know I have a sister?"

Sylvia shrugged. "Lucky guess?"

"Could be," Garth sounded doubtful.

"It makes more sense than anything else I've heard," Francis said decisively. "They're probably in Seattle this very minute laughing their heads off, knowing they have us worried."

"Sounds like the gang," John said darkly. "When they say they'll get you, they find a way."

"Well, that's a relief, then," Francis said as she

started walking toward the door. "No more need to watch out for the boogeyman."

"Hey, wait for me," one of the girls called out to Francis. "I want to go see those dresses, too."

Sylvia hesitated on the porch of the hardware store. The air was cold, and even the wood beneath her feet felt brittle. Sunlight strained through the thin clouds and emerged more white than yellow. There was no softness to this winter day. Garth had pulled the bus into the first space beside the door and he left the engine running.

"It'll be too cold otherwise," he said as he opened the bus door and stepped down.

"Remember to keep it in Park." Garth turned and gave instructions through the open door. One of the boys sat in the driver's seat. The other boys were huddled in the back of the bus talking. "If I see those wheels move an inch, you're out of there and standing with me out here in the cold."

Garth put his hands in the pockets of his wool coat and stood with his back hunched against the side of the bus. He turned and closed the door to the bus. He wanted to make small talk with Sylvia and he didn't want the boys listening. He'd already told the boys all of his conversational openers during the dance lessons and they would start to snicker when they recognized his feeble words in action.

"They going to be long?" Garth asked Sylvia as he nodded his head toward the girls inside the hardware store.

"Probably," Sylvia said as she rubbed her gloved

hands together. She could hear the excited squeals of the girls' voices. "But I'll see if I can hurry them up."

"No, don't. Won't hurt the boys to wait." Garth shrugged. "They're just anxious to start learning to drive that old tractor." Garth grinned at her. "I haven't told them yet that the wind will blow snow down their necks when they're sitting up that high and the rattle the old thing makes will leave them wishing they'd never made mention of driving."

Speaking of cold down the neck, Sylvia backed away from Garth slightly. If she looked up at him, the collar on her borrowed jacket bunched up and left a tunnel for cold air to race down her back. If she stepped back far enough, she could look up at him and still stay reasonably warm. Not that she had any need to look at him in the first place, she told herself. She hardly needed to worry about being polite. They were only waiting for the girls. They weren't even in a real conversation.

Garth grimaced when Sylvia stepped back. He was glad the boys weren't around to see him strike out on this conversation. The cold had turned Sylvia's lips pale and he could see her teeth start to chatter. But she looked beautiful to him. He wondered if the cold weather on the morning they had met had forever changed his definition of beauty. These days he was more likely to dream of women in a snowdrift than on a beach.

Sylvia knew Garth was looking at her. She didn't like it, but she refused to give in to vanity and wrap the soft wool scarf around her cheeks. She knew her face was pinched. Her nose was probably red and her cheeks blotchy. He was looking at her so intently, he must be remembering the day he'd found her half-frozen and slumped over in her car. She'd looked a fright then, too. He must be worried about her passing out again like that morning.

"I'm all right," she lied half-defiantly. "It's not really that cold."

She stepped even closer to the hardware store until she could feel the heat from inside. She glanced through the glass in the door and saw that the potbelly stove was still where she remembered it, square in the middle of the wooden floor. The two old men were still sitting around it and a game of checkers sat half-forgotten as the men turned to talk to the girls.

Garth glanced over his shoulder at the bus. Good. The windows had fogged up so no young eyes were watching him. He didn't need an audience for this. His moves were not smooth. He'd already proved that today. But as sure as a salmon swims north, he had to try. He stepped a little closer to Syliva. "But you must be a little cold. I could—"

Sylvia looked up at him in alarm and stepped back. "That's all right—I mean, we could always go in by the fire if you're cold."

"No, I'm fine." Garth backed away from her slightly. She was definitely prickly. He was only going to suggest that he stand in front of her so he would block the wind. How was he ever going to get close if she was afraid to get within ten inches of him? He had his Stetson pulled down to cover the tops of his ears and most of his forehead. His wool coat was unbuttoned and he had leather gloves sticking out of the pockets. "It's not bad. I've seen winter storms cold enough out to snap the phone lines."

Garth backed farther away and leaned against the bus. He hadn't broken that wild horse when he was seventeen without learning a trick or two. Give a wild animal room when you're making your move. "Besides, we haven't had a moment alone since morning."

"We don't need a moment alone."

"Of course we do. How else am I going to ask you to the dance?"

Garth stuck his hands in his pockets. He suddenly felt the chill in his bones, after all. What was it with women? He could feel the temperature drop another ten degrees in the air between them. Sylvia sure took her sweet time about answering his question.

Finally she spoke. "You don't have to ask me to the dance. I'm already going." She paused. "Everybody's going—even Jess."

"I know everybody's going," Garth said patiently. He might as well finish it up since he'd started this suicide mission. "But there's a difference between you just going because of course you're going, and you going with me."

Sylvia felt the cold air as she sucked in her breath. She had dreaded this moment. "I'm sorry, but I don't date."

Some men refuse to die. Today Garth decided he was one of them.

"But you already said you were going," Garth said smoothly. Patience wins in the end, he reminded himself. Don't take offense. Don't push. Don't let it die. "Technically you're probably going with me whether you agree to it or not, since I'm driving the bus."

"So we wouldn't be alone?" Sylvia asked in relief. She hated to point it out to him, but that didn't sound like a date at all. "All the kids will be there?"

"Well, they'll be sitting in the back of the bus," Garth agreed. "I was hoping you'd sit in the front with me."

"I guess I could do that." Sylvia shook her head slightly. It was, after all, little more than a seat assignment.

"Good. It's settled, then. It's a date." Garth pulled his Stetson down even farther on his head. "Oh, and Mrs. Buckwalter might want us to drive the pickup home. She's planning to have Jess drive it there with the lobster pots. But she won't want him to drive it home on account of his night vision being so poor."

"But then there'd just be the two of us." Sylvia frowned.

"Well, maybe there'll be a lobster or two still swimming around in the pots," Garth said cheerfully. "But they'll be in the back so you won't need to worry about them. That is, if we can find some pots to use—what with all the people in the county coming—" Garth left his worry dangling and, sure enough, Sylvia picked it up.

"Pots are the least of our problems," Sylvia said. "We don't even know what to do with lobsters! I can't believe she's just having them shipped here."

Garth congratulated himself. It appeared Sylvia was

even more afraid of those lobsters than she was of him.

"We'll figure it out. I asked Mrs. Buckwalter— they send instructions with the lobsters."

"A recipe?"

"Something like that. I figure if we could make the oatmeal from the directions on a box, we can do lobsters."

"The oatmeal had lumps."

"Well, the lobsters won't. They'll be perfect."

The door to the hardware store opened and, along with the warmth, Sylvia could smell a richly brewed coffee.

"That's almond-flavored." Sylvia turned to Garth in surprise. "Glory's favorite."

"Figured that's why Matthew bought a case of the stuff. They have it every day now. Matthew says it brings in the business. I tell him nobody needs to drink flavored coffee while they look through the catalog for feed supplements."

Two of the girls came out of the door carrying dresses covered with plastic bags.

"Mine's got gold sparkles on it," Paula announced proudly. "I'll look like a queen."

Francis came out the door, too, with two women behind her.

"Oh, Sylvia, meet Doris June and Margaret Ann. They're coordinating the dresses."

"I can't thank you enough," Sylvia said as she shook hands with the two attractive women.

"Well, don't thank us yet. We forgot the shoes."

"We might need to make a trip into Billings after all," Francis said.

"Let us see what we can do first," Doris June said. The blond-haired young woman looked comfortable in her denim jeans and a flannel shirt. "I'll call around. We should have enough shoes here in Dry Creek. It's just a matter of finding them."

The rest of the girls came out of the hardware store and rushed into the bus with their dresses. Garth stepped into the driver's seat and Sylvia found an empty seat midway back in the bus.

This really is going to be a Cinderella ball, Sylvia mused to herself as she looked around at the kids. Francis had called a hairstylist that worked in Miles City and the woman was going to come out tomorrow to help transform the girls into princesses. She looked at the boys. She wondered how Garth was coming along in his efforts to transform the boys into princes. After all, Cinderella could get to the ball with an old bus instead of a carriage, but it wouldn't be much fun if there wasn't a prince there to dance with her.

Meanwhile, nearby

Flint was careful to stay hidden until the bus drove away. There weren't many places to hide in Dry Creek, but he swore he knew them all. He'd been shocked last night to realize the little town had apparently not changed since he'd lived here twenty years ago.

Flint found he could still fit snugly into the crevice beside the chimney on the outside wall of Mrs.

Owen's house. He'd leaned back against the cold brick wall and had watched as the slow-moving bus had pulled up to the hardware store. The bus worried him. It wouldn't make much of a getaway vehicle. If he needed to get Francis away from here fast, he'd be better off on the back of the horse he'd rented in Miles City.

He hadn't had to fret for long. He saw Francis— his Francis—and all breath left him. She followed a group of teenage girls off the bus. It was as close as he'd been to Francis since he'd ridden his horse up to the shrub-lined border of Garth's ranch yesterday. Someone less observant would say Francis hadn't changed over the past twenty years. Her face held the same sweetness. Her step had the same regal gait. But his memory of Francis had been frozen in his heart for twenty years and he could pick out the small differences. The sadness that slumped her shoulders. The hesitancy that slowed her step just a little.

Maybe because everything else seemed unchanged in this little town, Flint had to fight the urge to go to her and enfold her in his arms. She belonged in his arms. Or she had, twenty years ago.

Flint had closed his eyes and taken a deep breath. The twenty years hadn't been erased. If he knew anything about women, he knew Francis had forgotten him years ago. There was no turning back time, not even in Dry Creek. When he'd opened his eyes, Francis had gone into the store.

Only her brother Garth and the other woman had stood outside. Flint would not have known Garth except for the pictures Francis had shown him long ago.

Flint could tell by the relaxed set of Garth's shoulders that the other man hadn't seen the tire marks that Flint had seen this morning while he rode his horse around the perimeter of Garth's ranch.

Flint knew that someone besides himself had been watching the ranch house from a distance last night. It looked as if it had been two men. They'd been amateurs. One had dropped a dozen cigarette butts and the cellophane wrappings of a candy bar. Flint had put everything in an evidence pack. Any professional would know not to leave trash lying around. The fact that the men were amateurs didn't comfort Flint. In fact, it made him even more worried. At least professionals knew what they were doing. Things had a way of getting out of control in the hands of amateurs.

Chapter Nine

❧

"It won't take more than another minute," Francis said as she pinned up the last turn of hem. Sylvia was wearing the dress, turning obediently so the hem would be even. The kids had willingly gone to bed early and Francis was doing the last-minute sewing on the dress Sylvia would be wearing tomorrow. Except for being too long, the dress fit well. "It's an old dress of mind. But it'll work for a maid-of-honor dress. Don't you think, Garth?"

Garth looked up from the magazine he'd been half reading. All evening he'd been fighting the urge to stare at Sylvia. He'd put a huge piece of wood in the fire earlier and the coals now gave off a yellow light that surrounded Sylvia where she stood. Sylvia had her black hair pinned back loosely, and the delicate arch of her exposed neck held a steady sweetness for Garth. Both women were concentrating on the hem and not paying any attention to him.

He was glad for the privacy. He wasn't sure his face could stand much scrutiny. He knew right where he wanted to kiss her. With a neck like that, she could be wearing a gunny sack instead of the soft pink dress and she'd be beautiful in his eyes. "It's perfect."

Francis nodded in satisfaction as she stuck the last pin into her pincushion and sat back to look up. "It was the dress I wore when I went to Vegas."

"Oh, but then—" Sylvia turned in surprise and looked at her new friend sitting at her feet with a tape measure looped around her arm "—are you sure you want me to wear it? Maybe you should keep it in the box. I could always wear one of the old prom dresses."

Francis shook her head. "I've lived with my ghost long enough. It's time to air the cobwebs out."

Francis fluffed the hem of Sylvia's dress one last time and then stood slowly. "In case you're wondering about doing the same thing, the ghost didn't bite."

Sylvia knew that was as close as Francis would come to asking about the past that haunted her own life. "Oh, but I've taken care of my ghost."

"Have you?" Francis asked softly as she put her pincushion back in her sewing box.

Sylvia didn't answer. Until recently she truly thought she had buried the ghost of her ex-husband. She could hardly remember anymore what his face looked like. She no longer had the urge to hide when she heard footsteps that sounded like his. The fear of violence remained, but she had used that to help others face the violence in their lives. She had thought it was enough. Now she was no longer sure.

"Sometimes it does help to talk," Garth said softly. He had long since laid down his magazine. The fire was dying down in the fireplace and Francis had turned off the overhead light before she started pinning on the dress. Garth hoped the shadows in the room would make Sylvia feel comfortable enough to talk.

"It doesn't always," Sylvia said as she turned so she faced both Garth and Francis. "Even friends don't always understand how it was."

"Friends would like to," Francis said softly. "Give us a chance."

Garth thought Sylvia wasn't going to answer. She turned to look into the fireplace. Only the coals were alive but the light they gave off was enough to silhouette Sylvia. She looked vulnerable as she stood with her back to him, but Garth knew he shouldn't go to her and hold her like he wanted to do. The battle within herself was one she needed to fight alone. He could not force her to feel safe with him.

Finally she spoke in low uneven words. "They called him Buck—his real name was Harry. I met him when I was sixteen. Ran off and married him at seventeen. I thought he was everything. It wasn't until we'd been married a year that his mean side came out. The first time he hit me I thought I'd done something wrong—I thought I wasn't doing it right—that if only I were a better housekeeper, a better wife—" She took a deep shaky breath. "If only I had a baby, I told myself it would make him happy. Then we could both be happy. I thought I'd never have a baby. Then one day it happened—I was pregnant.''

Sylvia lost herself in the telling of her story and stared into the fireplace for a long minute or two. ''I thought he'd finally be happy. That our lives would go back to the way they were when we had first married. I was two months along when he asked me for a beer one night. He'd been out and drinking but he wanted another one. We'd run out and I'd forgotten my ID earlier that day when I'd gone to the grocery store so they wouldn't sell me any. I told him we didn't have any and he started screaming. I tried to say I was sorry, but he started hitting me—'' Sylvia stopped and took a deep breath. Her voice came out flat. ''He beat me so bad, I woke up in the hospital. I lost the baby.''

Sylvia turned and looked at Francis and Garth. ''When I got out of the hospital, I left him.''

''I'm sorry,'' Garth murmured. He didn't know what else to say. All he wanted to do was protect her, and there was no way he could.

Sylvia watched Garth's face. His brown eyes darkened and she saw the pity in them. She'd seen the same kind of pity in the eyes of other friends. She lifted her chin. ''There's no need to be sorry for me— I mother many children now.''

''I'm not feeling sorry for you,'' Garth began. He knew he was walking through one of those minefields. He had to be careful. ''I'm sorry this all happened to you, and if I ever met up with that worthless husband of yours I'd show him a thing or two about—'' Garth stopped. Minefield. She had that little frown between her eyes. "But I'm assuming he was arrested—" Sylvia nodded and he continued gratefully. "And I believe in letting the law handle our problems." Her little frown went away. Unfortunately, the sweat that was gathering on Garth's forehead didn't. "What I mean to say is that I wish it had been different, and I would do anything if I could have been there to stop him."

"Thank you," Sylvia said softly as she stepped out of the circle of firelight.

Garth watched as Sylvia and Francis silently put away the sewing items. He wanted to stop Sylvia and talk to her, but the straightness of her back told him she didn't want to be comforted. For the time being, he had to be content that she had told him what happened.

Garth shifted in the chair he had dragged into the kitchen. He'd tried to go to sleep in his own bed, but with every creak in the old house, he was up and looking down the hallway. He finally decided he might as well come down to the kitchen and keep watch like his instincts were nudging him to do.

Everyone else might believe the Seattle gang was behind the telephone call, but the more he thought about it, the more he was convinced otherwise. It was the man's voice on the phone that made him uneasy. It hadn't been the voice of a teenager, or even that of a young man. It was the weary, stomped-on voice of a man who had been to hell and back and was only still talking through the sheer habit of it.

The voice belonged to a man that reminded Garth

of the man he'd been himself when he first came back from Asia. And even as violent as gang kids were today, they couldn't have seen the lifetime of weariness that would produce such a voice. No, the voice was combat hardened.

Strange that the fighting had been over for over twenty years and it was still the reason that he was sitting up on a cold winter night unable to let his suspicions rest.

He'd given up years ago on his hope that the scars would ever heal. He'd just accepted that he would always be lame inside. On that long drive over to Seattle, he and Matthew had shared life stories. They both had their scars, but Garth knew that, compared to his own, the scars haunting Matthew's soul were those of a choir boy. Garth doubted God would even want to look on his own scars, let alone heal them. That's why when Matthew had offered to pray for salvation in Garth's life, Garth had hedged.

Garth didn't trust mercy. And as for salvation, if he needed it, he'd have to find a way to earn it. That's always the way it had been for him. He'd learned that nothing came free in life. Of course, Matthew had argued with him on that. Ministers were big on hope. That was their job. Matthew had told him that it was no good patching up his own life. Only God could do it.

Garth didn't respond, but he knew at least part of what Matthew said was true. There was no escaping the mess Garth had made of his life. Patches wouldn't begin to cover it. All he had to do was remember what his wife had said. Until the day she died, his wife had complained bitterly about his failings.

Garth could only stand helpless by then. All that she said was true.

He'd come back from Vietnam a different man. He wasn't the man she'd dated in high school. The prisoner-of-war camp had almost killed him. He felt as if he knew things inside that no decent person should know and he had to walk very carefully or they'd all spill out. He hadn't wanted them to spill out on his wife so he had tread very carefully.

But bottling them up only made him seem cold. His wife couldn't see his distress and he couldn't explain it to her. She had accused him of turning into a hard-nosed old rancher just like his father, unwilling to bend in life for any reason. Garth had flinched at her words, but he hadn't cracked. It was true. He supposed that's why he couldn't believe in mercy. His father didn't believe in it, either.

"What you need," Matthew had said that day driving back from Seattle, "is a new skin—"

Garth couldn't argue with that. What was it Matthew had said again? Garth tried to remember, especially because he knew that if he couldn't call the words to mind he'd be awake all night. The partial words would be like a phrase of a song lodged in his brain. The only solution was to go to his office and look at the Bible Matthew had marked and then given to him.

Well, he never was a man to put off unpleasant things, Garth said to himself as he swept off the blankets and stood up. His feet were bare and the linoleum was cold on his feet. He quickly sat down again and pulled on a pair of wool socks.

On his way back into the kitchen with the Bible in his hand, he turned on the small lamp he'd placed by his chair. He opened the Bible to the marker Matthew had left. There it was—*Mark* 2:21, 22: "No one sews a piece of unshrunk cloth on an old garment. If he does, the patch tears away from it, the new from the old, and a worse tear is made. And no one puts new wine into old wineskins; if he does, the wine will burst the skins, and the wine is lost, and so are the skins; but new wine is for fresh skins."

Now what did that mean? Garth supposed Matthew was trying to tell him it would do no good to patch up his life—that he would only mess it up if he tried—and that what he needed was a whole new one instead. He supposed Matthew could get a few votes on that if he put it to the people around here. He couldn't help but wonder what Sylvia would think of him if he was a new man.

Likely it wouldn't make much difference, he told himself sternly, as he walked over to the frosted windows and peered out into the night darkness. She still wouldn't trust him enough to lean back into his touch. He felt his fist curl. He'd told Sylvia he would have let the police handle her ex-husband if he knew him, but it wasn't altogether true. He might let the police pick up the pieces, but he'd make sure the rotten excuse for a man knew someone had gut-punched him before he gave him over.

Garth opened the door to breathe in a gulp of icy air. He'd never be able to sleep if he thought of Sylvia's ex-husband. He stepped out onto the porch in his stocking feet. It was peaceful out here. He could almost hear the groaning of the ice forming in the water tanks out by the barn. They'd need to crack the ice in the morning so the cattle could drink.

He looked down the long dirt road that connected his house to the gravel country road. There was a thin layer of snow from earlier in the night that shone on the permanent ruts in the road. No tire marks disturbed the snow. No intruders were out there.

He looked down at the bunkhouse where the girls were staying. Sylvia had taken a flashlight and walked down there not more than an hour ago. All of the windows were dark in the girls' bunkhouse, and he glanced over at the boys' bunkhouse to check it. The lights were out there, as well. He felt a sudden wave of protective contentment as he looked at the two bunkhouses. There was no doubt about it. Those kids were growing on him.

He smiled to himself. He'd have to give another dance lesson to the boys in the morning. They wouldn't like it, but they would thank him when they were terror-stricken tomorrow night on the dance floor.

He looked down at his watch. There was barely enough light from the open door behind him to see the hands, but he could make out the time. It was two o'clock. He turned around. He'd better get some sleep if he expected to dance until midnight tomorrow.

A muffled kick against the outside kitchen door woke Garth. Startled, he grabbed the baseball bat he kept beside the chair and looked around. The morning light was gray but it streamed in through the windows strongly. Nothing looked out of place. The box of oatmeal stood in the middle of the table. The counters were swept clear except for the plastic canisters for flour, sugar and coffee that were supposed to be there.

He looked down at his watch. It was almost seven, but they'd planned a late breakfast. The alarms in the bunkhouse wouldn't be ringing for another half hour. And if it was Sylvia or one of the others at the door, he would see their form in the frosted windowpanes at the top of the door. They would have no reason to hide.

No, something was wrong. He had the sense that his ears had heard other scuffling sounds before the kick. Well, maybe not scuffling sounds, more like soft grunts and the scraping of soft-soled shoes.

He picked up the phone that he had pulled into the kitchen from his office last night before he settled himself in the chair. The dial tone was still active. That relieved his fears. Even an amateur would know to cut the phone lines if they were up to something. He wondered if he should dial down to the girls' bunkhouse and tell Sylvia to keep the girls inside or if that would just frighten them and make them want to run up to the house.

No, he was best to keep them out of it. Besides, they weren't in danger. It was Francis who had been threatened.

He tiptoed to the bottom of the stairs and called softly, "Fannie."

He didn't want to open that door until he knew

Francis was all right. He knew about traps that baited the curious. "Fannie?" he called again. He didn't want to leave the kitchen door unguarded or he would climb the stairs and wake Francis himself.

"What?" A grumble came from Francis's room.

"Nothing," Garth called back up, relieved.

He hefted the baseball bat onto his shoulder and walked softly back into the kitchen. He adjusted the bat and then hesitated. He supposed it was possible the boys were playing a trick on him. They were that age. He didn't want to scare them spitless by coming at them with a bat. He lowered the bat to his side.

The lock snapped quietly open but the doorknob whined slightly as he twisted it. He needed to give it a squirt of WD-40.

He took a deep breath. Surprise was half of his ammunition in this operation. He swung the door open quickly and stepped into position with his bat. Well, he amended his actions. He tried to step into position, but something rolled against his legs.

"What the—?" He stared down at what looked like a dirty ball of human arms and legs at his feet. "How the—?"

He counted heads. There were only two. With all of the arms and legs, he thought there would be more. But no, there were just the two. One was a pixie-faced young woman with very tousled short brown hair. The other was a man so indignant, Garth feared for the poor fellow's heart. Both of them were gagged with red bandannas and tied together with rope so new, it fairly squeaked. Garth suspected he'd find his new coil missing from the barn wall when he went out there later.

Garth doubted anyone could have tied them into the tangle of rope they now found themselves in. They must have twisted and turned their way into the ball of limbs at his feet.

"Who—?" Garth mumbled again in amazement until he saw the irritation blaze up in the man's eyes. Whoever was lying at his feet was obviously not used to finding himself unable to talk.

"In a second." Garth answered the man's demand as he bent down and briefly patted both of them for weapons. It didn't make the man any happier, but Garth wasn't taking any chances. The two had been rolling around in the snow and flakes of it came off in Garth's hand. Only then did he lift his eyes and look farther outside than the porch.

"What—?" He was speechless.

The day was overcast and the light was gray. But even in the half-light Garth would need to be totally blind not to see the small airplane that sat serenely between his house and his barn. He blinked and looked again. No, it definitely was a plane. A small two-seater plane to be sure, but a plane nonetheless. He would have suspected it was a mirage, but he saw Sylvia walking out of the bunkhouse and staring at the plane, too.

Garth looked back down at the tangle at his feet. And then he looked up again at the plane and noticed the wide path in the snow that led from the plane to the door. He looked down at his feet again. Would you believe that? Those two had managed to form a ball and roll their way to his doorstep. They'd even hobbled up the steps somehow.

He needed to untie one of the bandanna gags before he had any hope of getting his questions answered. The only decision left to make was which bandanna to loosen. The man looked like he'd as soon spit at the world as talk to anyone so Garth decided to lean down and untie the gag on the woman first.

"Oh, thank you," the woman said as he lifted the gag out of her mouth. She took a deep breath and ran her tongue around her lips. "Whoever washed that bandanna last didn't get all of the soap out of it. Too short of a rinse cycle I think."

The bound man grunted at her in annoyance.

"Well, they didn't," she turned to him and said indignantly. "And I don't think you would have liked it, either. Not that you probably even know what laundry soap smells like. I bet you've never done a load of wash in your life."

The man glared at her.

Garth relaxed and smiled at the man. "Quarrel with the wife?"

"Oh, no." The woman seemed genuinely alarmed. "We're not married. I mean—no, we're not married. I work for him, that's all."

The man grunted again.

"Well, I did work for him," the woman continued a little uncertainly. And then she added defiantly, "Actually, I work for his mother and I'm not even sure he can fire me."

The man grunted again.

Garth looked down at the man a little warily. He

supposed he needed to untie the man's gag. He just wasn't sure he wanted to witness the argument that seemed in progress.

"Who are they?" Sylvia stepped onto the porch.

"That's what I'm going to find out," Garth said as he eyed the ropes on the man.

"I'm Jenny," the woman offered as she smiled up at Sylvia.

"And I'm Sylvia." She knelt down and pulled off her gloves to work at the knot behind Jenny's back. "Whoever managed a knot like this?"

Garth's fingers stopped. He looked down at the man's face. The man was boiling mad. Garth knew that once he untied the man's gag, Garth wouldn't get a word in edgewise with Sylvia this morning. And he wanted to reassure her that everyone was safe.

"Sorry. It won't be long," Garth said as he abandoned the man's gag and moved his hands over to help Sylvia's struggle with her knot. Sylvia's fingers were still warm from being inside her gloves. But she did not seem to mind the cold of Garth's fingers as their fingers worked together on the knot.

This is the way it should be, Garth told himself. He and Sylvia working together. When the rope unknotted, Garth gave Sylvia's hand a squeeze. The skin on her hands was chilly now, but still soft as a summer peach. He held her hand for a second or two longer.

"What are you doing?" Sylvia asked with a trace of panic in her voice.

"Congratulating you." Garth tried to be nonchalant. "Shaking your hand sort of. You did a good job untying that knot."

Sylvia relaxed. "Oh, well, thank you."

Garth looked down at the gagged man at his feet. For a man who was gagged and couldn't talk, this one sure had a cocky, knowing look in his eyes.

"Well, you're not doing any better, Casanova," Garth mumbled low in the man's ear as he bent behind him to untie the bandanna.

The hard footsteps on the floor behind him told Garth he had more company.

"What's going on here?" Mrs. Buckwalter demanded as she marched across the kitchen floor. She had a gray wool robe pulled securely around herself and several pink plastic curlers in her hair. Even in the robe, she'd taken time to put on her regular shoes.

Garth had a sudden wish he had so prepared. The snow that had shaken off his two guests was melting and it was making his socks wet.

"What is it?" A lighter voice came from the stairs as Francis came into view.

"We've got company" was all Garth could think of to say.

"Well, bless my heart," Mrs. Buckwalter exclaimed as she walked closer and peered at the woman. "It's Jenny!"

Then Mrs. Buckwalter got close enough to see around Garth as he knelt by the couple. Her face went white and then rosy. "And Robert!"

Garth's fingers stopped in midtwist. "You know them?"

"Well, of course, I know them," Mrs. Buckwalter

said indignantly. "I've been telling you about them all week. That's Robert—" she pointed at the man as though that explained everything "—and my chef, Jenny."

Sylvia noticed the cold for the first time since she'd walked out of the bunkhouse this morning and saw the small plane sitting there so innocently. "R-Robert," she stammered. She stopped trying to unknot the rope behind Jenny's hands. "You don't mean—"

Sylvia looked in dread at Mrs. Buckwalter, but the older woman was beaming.

"That's right," Mrs. Buckwalter said proudly as she adjusted one of her curlers as if it were a royal crown. "Robert, my son."

"Robert Buckwalter," Sylvia repeated woodenly. *Dear Lord, we're doomed. He wasn't supposed to come. He was supposed to be traipsing about Europe someplace.*

Sylvia shook herself mentally. If she looked panic-stricken, he'd close them down for sure, thinking she was up to no good. She forced herself to smile. "Well, welcome."

Robert Buckwalter grunted. Sylvia's heart sank even more. He didn't look too happy.

"I know this isn't the way you're used to being greeted," Sylvia continued nervously. "Not that, of course, we had anything to do with this. We would never—"

Sylvia did a quick mental check wondering if any of the kids would tie up two strangers. No, she assured herself, of course not. She continued more emphatically. "We would never greet anyone this way. And we'll be happy to show you around as soon as you're untied and have had breakfast—" Sylvia's voice faltered. She remembered they were having oatmeal. *Dear Lord, at least let me get this right. No lumps, please.*

"Now," Garth said as he sat back on his heels and watched as Robert rubbed his mouth. The gag was off. "Tell us what happened." He looked at Jenny. "Both of you."

"There was a man," Jenny began.

Robert snorted. "Not just any man. A man about five feet eleven inches tall. I'd say one hundred and seventy pounds. Wiry. Maybe forty years old. Had some karate skills, at least that's what it looked like to me. He never actually made those kind of moves on us—"

"He didn't have to," Jenny interrupted and glared at Robert. "You wanted to surrender right away. You wouldn't even fight for what is yours."

"The day I risk death for a planeload of lobsters is the day I—"

"Lobsters!" Sylvia gasped. Her nightmare had arrived.

"Well, just because you have more gold than King Midas doesn't mean you should just throw it away," Jenny scolded. "Lobsters aren't cheap. Some people don't have money to just throw them away like they were sardines."

"Back to the man," Garth reminded them patiently. Robert and Jenny looked at him blankly. He repeated. "The man who tied you up. Did he say why he did that?"

"Well, I assumed he was going to rob us," Robert said indignantly.

Sylvia went limp with relief. Someone had stolen the lobsters. Hallelujah!

"He didn't even ask for your wallet," Jenny countered. "You half threw it at him." She pointed over to the plane. "And it's still lying there in the snow."

Everyone turned to look at the black square on the snowy ground.

"Well, if it wasn't robbery, what was it?" Robert looked up at Garth blankly.

"I don't know," Garth said grimly. But as sure as he had breath in his body, he'd find out.

"He just seemed to come out of nowhere when we landed," Robert said. "At first I thought he was confused. Said something about getting—or was it not getting?—someone. Frank or something."

"Francis," Francis herself said softly. She looked at Garth bleakly. "There is someone out to get me."

"Well, maybe I have the name wrong." Robert looked up at Francis. "Or maybe it wasn't a name at all. Maybe it was something like frankly—maybe he said he was going to get us frankly."

"But he didn't," Francis pointed out softly. "He didn't get you at all."

"Well, he did tie us up," Robert protested weakly. "Maybe that's all he wanted."

Robert looked at Garth. Sylvia saw the look Garth gave him in return. Neither man believed anyone had said "frankly."

Chapter Ten

"Preserves?" Jenny asked as she lifted up one of Garth's juice glasses. She'd filled it earlier with some European apricot preserves that made Sylvia's mouth water even before she saw the fluffy biscuits that Jenny plucked from the oven.

Breakfast was later than usual because Garth and his hands had searched every building on the ranch looking for the man who had tied up Jenny and Robert last night. They spent two hours searching, but they didn't find anyone or any signs that anyone unusual had been around.

Jenny had made her first batch of baking-powder biscuits for the search party. She was taking the biscuits out of the oven just as they all came into the kitchen. The heat from the oven and the cold from the open door made a hazy steam.

"Whoever it is, he's gone," Garth had announced as he unwound the scarf from around his head.

Sylvia stared. That was the first time she'd seen Garth go outside without his Stetson. Instead of the hat, he'd wound that scarf around his head and neck and anchored it with a John Deere baseball cap.

"Must have been a—what do you call them here— one of your rustlers," Robert Buckwalter concluded. Robert had changed out of his snow-encrusted Armani suit and Francis had given him some of Garth's clothes—a red-and-gray flannel shirt and a pair of jeans. He'd worn a parka over them and joined the men in the search.

Garth only grunted at the theory and looked sideways at the women. "Doubt it."

"We don't need to be protected," Sylvia said indignantly. "You can tell us if there's trouble."

"When you're on my ranch, you're my responsibility, " Garth replied, tight-lipped. "You don't need to worry about trouble."

"I'm not a child," Sylvia snapped back. "I can take care of myself."

"Biscuits anyone?" Jenny interrupted and held a platter high. "I've got butter and apricot jam. If everyone finds a chair we'll eat."

"You're on my Christmas card list forever," Sylvia told Jenny as she bit into another apricot-topped biscuit. The two of them were sitting alone at the table after everyone else had finished breakfast. "You've saved us from lumpy oatmeal and half-burnt roast."

Jenny had come prepared with several boxes of food in addition to the lobsters.

Jenny laughed. "Well, I love to cook. And these

kids—they're an easy audience to please. I promised to bring them pastrami sandwiches for lunch while they're decorating the barn and you'd think I'd offered them pure gold.''

"They'd probably trade gold for some good food after my cooking," Sylvia said ruefully. "If there were any fast-food places around they'd be staging a mutiny already. I can't tell you how happy I am you're here to help.''

"Well, it's good to have your cooking appreciated," Jenny said unhappily as she looked over at Robert.

Sylvia followed her gaze. Robert and his mother were standing in a corner of the kitchen and talking softly. Sylvia watched them closely, but it didn't look as if they were arguing. She was glad about that. So far, Robert hadn't said anything to her about the money his mother had donated to her center. But then maybe he was just letting her have her last meal in peace. She looked back at Jenny. "Well, if he doesn't appreciate your cooking, he must have had all his taste buds surgically removed.''

Jenny smiled. "It's not that—it's just that he's eaten in some of the finest restaurants in Europe— from Paris to Rome. I've never even been to Europe. I can't compete with that.''

Sylvia had been around enough teenagers to recognize the signs. "Why is it I have a feeling we're not only talking about food here?''

"We might as well only be talking about food for all the good it will ever do me," Jenny said forthrightly. "But I'm not one to sit around moping over what I can't have.'' She pushed her chair back from the table. ''Especially not when I've got one hundred people coming for dinner.''

''Well, I for one completely adore you—and your cooking,'' Sylvia said, and then added ruefully, ''Besides, if you weren't here, I'd be trying to buy all the cream cheese in Miles City so I could make something resembling wedding appetizers on a stick.''

''Cream cheese rolled in those paper-thin ham slices with a toothpick stuck in them?'' Jenny guessed and grimaced.

''With chopped olives,'' Sylvia added, and then snuck another peek at the Buckwalters in the corner. ''Oh, no.'' The Buckwalters were clearly in a heated discussion.

''Don't worry,'' Jenny said, giving her hand a pat as she stood. ''He might not notice me, but he's a fair man. He won't just pull the rug out from under you without seeing you have someplace else to stand. And in the meantime, we have radishes to turn into roses,'' Jenny said as she gestured toward the kitchen counter.

''And don't forget the ice sculpture—'' Mrs. Buckwalter turned from her discussion with her son and beamed at the other women. ''I want to do something special—'' The older woman stopped and then glanced out the window she was near. ''Oh, dear, what's that?''

Sylvia heard a deep, rattling throttle and then the hard clicking sounds of boots walking across the porch. She saw Garth's silhouette through the door windowpanes before he opened the door and came into the kitchen.

Garth had his gray Stetson hat tilted back as though he had been concentrating on looking at something and then had forgotten to change the angle of his hat. He wore a wool jacket, but it was unbuttoned. His face had settled into lines of tiredness, but he was clean-shaven. At the moment, he looked exasperated. "Anybody see my ear muffs?"

"I think one of the girls borrowed them," Francis said as she walked into the kitchen from the living room. "I didn't think you ever used them so I thought it would be all right."

"It is," Garth said curtly. "I'm just looking for something to cut the noise. When these boys gun the motor on that old tractor, you can hear them in the next county."

It was a good two hours later before Sylvia had the kids loaded into the bus and delivered to Dry Creek so they could start decorating the barn. It was the same barn that Sylvia had seen decorated for the Christmas pageant a couple of months earlier. The wood inside had been scrubbed to a light pine shine before the pageant and even the rafters had been dusted. The barn would do justice to the dance to come.

"Throw me another roll of that rose paper," K.J. shouted from where he stood on a ladder underneath the hayloft at the back of the barn. They had three colors of crepe paper streamers—rose, light pink and white. They were draping them from the rafters in a crisscross pattern and were hanging big white wedding bells in the middle.

"When do we get to break out the sandwiches?" John asked for the second time in fifteen minutes. He was pushing a big, industrial broom.

"But it's only ten o'clock. Besides, we're not going to eat the sandwiches here," Sylvia explained again. "Matthew said we could go over to the hardware store for lunch. It's warmer there and he's going to heat us up some hot cocoa."

"Sure hope those heaters kick in before tonight," one of the girls said as she wrapped her sweater more closely around her. "Those dresses will be cold without heat."

"The heaters will work." Garth walked toward them. He had flecks of straw on his wool jacket and the headband of his Stetson. "I tried them out when Mrs. Hargrove first had her idea, and they warmed up the place nice—just took them a few hours."

"Hey, can somebody help with these tables?" one of the ranch hands called from the front of the barn.

Garth had offered the services of his ranch hands to help set up for the wedding dance tonight. He said it was a slow work week for them anyway. But Sylvia noticed that the hands took turns being stationed at the entrance to the barn, and from the way they kept looking outside it was clear their instructions were to be security guards.

"I've got the tablecloths for them," Francis said as she turned from where she was helping two of the girls twist the crepe paper. She looked to the front of the barn where two of the ranch hands were moving a long unfolded banquet table. "Just set it down and I'll snap the legs up on it. There's a trick to it."

"I'll come help you," Sylvia offered.

"No," Garth began and Sylvia turned to him again. "I mean—I was hoping you could help me."

"You?"

Garth nodded and then said in a low voice, "I need your help with something in this book—" He gestured to a small green book that was in his pocket. Sylvia looked but she didn't see a title. "I don't want the boys to see so I thought maybe you could help."

"Of course," Sylvia said. She always encouraged learning and if Garth needed something explained from a book she was honored he would ask her. "I applaud learning—"

"Well, it's not exactly that kind of learning—" Garth warned as he gestured for her to follow him and started to walk toward the back of the barn.

"It doesn't need to be highbrow," Sylvia said with a wave of her hand as she followed him. "All learning is important in the eyes of God."

Garth grunted. "Remember that."

Sylvia continued as though he hadn't interrupted her. She thought she was getting the hang of being around Garth. If she tried to picture him as one of the boys she tutored, she'd be all right. She had a full stock of learning platitudes. "We are what we learn. I'm sure I can help you with what you need. I may not understand it. I don't know much about farming. Or animals, really—unless they're cats, of course. But I can help with the words."

"Well, it's not so much the words—" Garth said as he stopped.

Sylvia looked up. They were standing at the foot of the ladder leading up to the hayloft. The steps up were steep, but that's not why Sylvia hesitated. The rest of the barn was brightly lit, but the light in the hayloft was dim.

"I can look at the book here," Sylvia offered.

"But the boys—" Garth nodded with his head to where the boys were standing.

Sylvia followed his gaze. Sure enough the boys were watching them. "Well, really, I don't see what it matters if they see—"

Garth looked mildly offended. "They need to think I know what I'm doing."

Men and their pride, Sylvia thought in exasperation. "Well, all right. We'll climb up there and read it. Although the light is much better down here."

"We won't need good light. It's mostly the pictures I need help with," Garth said as he stepped aside for her. "Ladies first."

Sylvia had one foot on the first step, but she turned around. "It's not geometry, is it? I'm afraid I'm not very good at geometry."

"Well, there is somewhat of a triangle involved. But go ahead—we'll work it out."

Sylvia stood in the center of the hayloft and looked down at the book Garth held open.

"That's not a triangle at all," she accused.

"Sure it is," Garth said as his finger traced the dance step in his book. "One. Two."

There were no windows in the hayloft and the only

light filtered in from the opening at the front of the hayloft where a space was left for lowering bales down to the cattle below. The sweet smell of dried alfalfa surrounded them.

"But those are dance steps. And we already tried dancing. You don't need my help. You've been teaching the boys to dance already. I saw you."

"I haven't taught them dipping," Garth said as he took off his hat and laid it on one of the hay bales that lined the center of the hayloft.

"You don't need to take off your hat."

"A gentleman always takes off his hat when he dances with a lady."

Garth watched the emotions play across Sylvia's face. He was glad he hadn't just asked her straight out to dance with him again. The answer would have been no. But he knew she wanted the boys to learn dipping. He wondered if she wanted it enough to spend more time in his arms. "You'll need to dance with me anyway tonight. The kids will never rest until we've danced."

"I thought maybe I could dance with one of the boys—"

Garth shook his head. "As I remember it, at wedding parties the bride and groom dance and then the wedding party takes to the floor."

Sylvia looked at him blankly.

"That's us. Matthew asked me to be his best man. And you're Glory's maid of honor. We make up the wedding party."

"But we don't have any music."

Garth patted his other pocket and brought out a

transistor radio. "It'll be scratchy, but it'll give us the beat."

Sylvia still hesitated.

"You don't need to be afraid of me," Garth said gently as he opened his arms. "I'd never hurt you."

"I'm not afraid of you," Sylvia protested stiffly as she stepped into his arms. "It's only a dance."

Garth didn't realize how tense he'd been until he felt Sylvia in his arms. Suddenly everything was all right again. His butterfly woman was in his arms. She floated with him. Their shoes brushed aside the wisps of straw as they danced.

"One. Two." Sylvia began to count.

Garth smiled. She could recite the dictionary for all he cared. The soft murmur of her voice warmed him. The sounds of a waltz scratched away on his radio. He was going to have to find out who ran the programming at that station and send them a thank-you ham. Maybe even a side of beef. Not that he needed the radio. His heart made its own music.

"Shouldn't we be dipping?"

Sylvia's question broke his reverie. Apparently his was the only heart that had been making music. Sylvia was looking at him suspiciously, as though she knew he'd used the dipping as an excuse to get her in his arms again.

"Just getting warmed up," Garth said defensively. Didn't the woman have any patience? "A guy can't just race around the dance floor and then dip—that's not very romantic. He has to wait for the moment when the music is just right and all."

"It's only for practice. We don't need a moment."

"Well, we do need the right rhythm."

"I'll count it out for us. One. Two. Three—" Sylvia drew out the last number expectantly and then paused. "You were supposed to dip on three."

"Nobody says I have to dip on three." Garth let go of Sylvia's hand and reached into his pocket that held the book. She slowed down and was going to pull away, but he pulled her back with his other arm. "Uh-uh, no need to stop. I'm just checking the directions."

Garth took his time looking at the diagram. "The woman in the picture is dancing a lot closer to the man than you're standing to me."

"A couple doesn't need to stand close to dance."

"Well, they need to at least be in the same vicinity," Garth said. His feet were still moving and Sylvia was still following him. He supposed he should be thankful for that much. He didn't know how much longer she'd take his lead. "Especially if they're going to—" Garth held his breath, took a firm hold on Sylvia's waist and dipped her.

Sweet Lord above! Garth felt his heart rise to his throat. There'd been nothing in the diagram about the way Sylvia's eyes would look at him when he dipped her. Maybe it was only the surprise. But she looked at him like she was seeing him for the first time in a dream and liking every wrinkle on his sorry face. Her eyes only held him until she let out a soft kitten breath. Then he noticed her lips. They were slightly parted, as if she was going to say something but couldn't quite remember what it was.

Garth told himself he was only human. What

choice did a man have? He bent his head slightly and kissed her. He knew he should keep the kiss light, but her lips were soft and he felt a jackhammer beating inside. A man had to take his chances in life. He deepened the kiss and tasted her sweetness. His last thought was that he could die a happy man.

It was Sylvia who pulled away. "That's not in the directions."

Garth pulled himself back to reality. "Huh?"

"The kiss," Sylvia said distinctly. "I'm sure that's not in the directions."

Sylvia was still dipped but she was no longer looking up at him as if he was a dream. The fact is, she was looking at him more like he was an annoying nightmare that wouldn't go away no matter how much she frowned at him.

"It's implied," Garth said curtly as he straightened out his arm and brought Sylvia back to her dancing position.

"It better not be implied when you teach it to the boys," Sylvia scolded.

Garth didn't answer her. He usually knew what kind of ground he stood on, but with Sylvia he wasn't sure whether he was on granite or quicksand. Her cheeks were flushed and he could swear she'd kissed him back with all of the fervor he'd felt in his own hammering heart. But maybe he was mistaken. Maybe he'd been so moved by the kiss, he'd only convinced himself she was responding.

"We'd better get back downstairs." Sylvia drew away from him.

Garth let Sylvia float out of his arms and then he turned to pick up his hat. "You'll have to dance with me tonight, you know," he reminded her brusquely. "And I'll need to dip you to prove to the boys that I know how to do it."

"Well, you don't need to dip me. You could dance with someone else and dip them."

"You wouldn't want me to dip one of the girls."

"You're right on that," Sylvia said emphatically. "I don't even want you to dance with one of them unless you dance with all of them. But you're welcome to dip Mrs. Buckwalter."

Garth grunted. He doubted Mrs. Buckwalter would like that any better than he would.

Meanwhile, in the shadows of Dry Creek

Flint was cursing the cold. Why would anyone want to kidnap anyone in weather like this? He was wearing a beat-up brown parka and thermal underwear, but his bones were so cold he was afraid they'd start to rattle when he walked. The only saving grace, he ruefully admitted to himself, was that at least his legs were too cold to protest the bruising they'd taken last night on that horse. He'd been told her name was Honey. He'd hoped the name would sweeten her. It hadn't. Still, she got the job done.

He and Honey had been up all night guarding Garth's ranch. Flint knew the rustlers were out there. He'd even gotten close enough to two of them last night to hear them talking about orders to bring in the package soon. He'd hidden behind some low trees near Garth's west fence. He'd tied Honey up down the fence and lain on his belly on the freezing ground for a good half hour listening to the two men complain.

The two men hadn't mentioned whether the package they were going to ship was a certain woman or a truckload of cattle. It was annoying to wait so long and find out nothing but the kind of corn pads they used on their feet. He'd stopped listening when he heard the plane just before dawn. The two men scurried to their pickup like frightened toads in a thunderstorm when they heard the growing hum.

Flint thought the people in the plane must be involved, but the man and woman were more tourists than anything. They were deep in an argument when he pulled them from the plane. The only way he could stop the bickering was to put gags in their mouths.

Flint shook his head. Why would anyone fly into Montana in the middle of winter with a stack of live lobsters? It was the lobsters as much as the bickering that convinced him they were innocents.

Flint rubbed his gloved hands over his arms and shivered. Honey might be a pain, but he missed her all the same. She was the only breathing thing he'd talked to since he came to Montana.

By now she would be warm and cozy, content with her bale of hay. He'd bedded her down in an abandoned chicken coop that still stood on the farm just outside of town. He'd inherited the farm from his grandmother when she died twenty years ago.

That property is what had brought him to Dry Creek long ago, and he'd never been able to sell it. The Montana winters managed to kill off the weeds each year or it would be overgrown by now. As far as he knew, no one but gophers ever visited the place anymore.

Chapter Eleven

The headlights on the bus showed up the ruts in the gravel road leading away from Garth's ranch. The lights weren't bright enough to dim the winter stars in the black night, however, and Sylvia looked out to admire them. She had to admit that Cinderella's coach couldn't have been more magical than this bus as it slowly ground its way to the ball.

Sylvia sat in the front seat, the one just behind Garth.

"I've saved this seat for you," Garth had said as Sylvia had stepped into the bus.

Sylvia was the last one to board the bus and she had assumed she'd need to squeeze in somewhere left over.

"Shouldn't you give that one to Francis?" Sylvia looked down the rows of seats. "She's carrying those bowls for lobster butter. They'll ride better in front."

The smell of Ivory soap was unmistakable inside

the bus. The ranch hands were seated at the back of the bus with their hair slicked down and their hats in their hands. And the kids—she hardly recognized the kids. The girls were glamorous under their wraps. Up-swirled hair and sparkling earrings peeked out from under serviceable parkas and thick jackets. Even the boys managed to look younger than they did in their street clothes.

"Francis and her bowls are fine next to Mrs. Buck-walter," Garth said patiently.

"But—" Sylvia looked at the front seat again. Someone had spread a fluffy white blanket open on the seat. And in the middle of the blanket lay a cor-sage of pink rosebuds laced about with baby's breath. Her eyes flew up to Garth's. "But—"

"A lady deserves a rose or two," Garth said softly.

Sylvia felt her breath catch. She hadn't stopped to take a good look at Garth this evening. She smelled the faint scent of a pine aftershave and noticed the boyish smile on his face. He was wearing a black tuxedo with cowboy boots and a wool hunter's jacket. The pressed white of his shirt made his tan look golden. He had on a different Stetson—this one a black so smooth, it looked like velvet.

"But where did you get it?" Sylvia knew there was no florist in Dry Creek. He would have needed to go to Miles City. That must have been where Garth went this afternoon. "I hope you were going for supplies, too."

Garth didn't answer directly. "Sometimes a special lady deserves something special no matter how much time it takes away from the chores." His voice poured over her spine and made it tingle. "And a gentleman makes it a point to see that those times come around."

"Oh." Sylvia snapped herself out of it. She was being a ninny. When Garth said the word *gentleman* she finally understood. He was showing the boys how to behave in a social situation. She felt herself relax. She was an object lesson in his role playing. She didn't need to worry. They were just team teaching. There was no need for the tingling in her spine. She was little more than a map on the wall in his classroom.

"Well, thank you. The corsage is quite lovely. Every lady—or girl—would be pleased with such a gift." Sylvia picked up the corsage and turned it so that the kids could see. She hadn't even lifted the roses up high before the boys started to stomp and applaud.

Sylvia turned back to Garth in satisfaction. "That worked very well. You're a natural teacher. Brilliant idea."

Garth opened his mouth and closed it again. What did she mean by "That worked very well?" By the sounds of it, it hadn't worked at all. He'd wanted to get a glimpse of the Sylvia he had dipped earlier. Instead, he got the congratulations of a schoolmarm.

Well, he assured himself, they hadn't begun to dance. She'd look at him with dreams in her eyes before the evening was over, or his name wasn't Garth Elkton.

It wasn't until he was parking the bus in front of the café in Dry Creek that Garth remembered his real name technically wasn't Garth Elkton. His birth certificate listed him as Gerald Elkton, in honor of a grandfather. He hoped that wasn't a bad omen.

Sylvia forced her eyes to look straight ahead. She was standing with her back to the entire population of Dry Creek, listening as the vows were read again to Glory and Matthew. It was a solemn moment. A holy moment before God. She had no business letting her mind, or her eyes, wander to the man standing just slightly behind Matthew. Just because the best man had the bad manners to let his eyes wander over to her instead of focusing on the couple reciting their vows was no reason for her to relax her attention or her spine. She'd count the buttons on the back of Glory's dress if she needed. Anything to keep her eyes in place.

"When it comes to better or worse," the pompous voice of deputy sheriff Carl Wall sounded forth. The deputy had an open Bible in his hand and an empty holster at his side. "I figure the two of you have already come to the bad part and waded through it pretty blamed good—so here's hoping that's all done and behind you. I wouldn't think there'd be more folks out to kill you."

Deputy Wall had offered to read the lines for Glory and Matthew as they re-affirmed their vows in the hearing of all of Dry Creek. When Mrs. Hargrove had protested that she'd not have an armed man read from the Bible, the deputy had pulled his gun out of his holster and set it on the counter at the hardware store. When she'd protested he wasn't a minister, he'd said that aside from Matthew, he was the only recognized official in the whole town of Dry Creek.

"And the minister can't marry himself," Deputy Wall had said emphatically.

"It wouldn't be right."

Mrs. Hargrove hadn't had an answer to that one.

"Besides, I have a uniform," Deputy Wall had continued. "I'll look good in the pictures. Hear they might send a photographer out from Billings. We'd want a good picture. Do Dry Creek proud."

Mrs. Hargrove had given in and Deputy Wall had been at it for fifteen minutes now. Sylvia thought he sounded as if he was reading a prisoner his rights rather than reading parts of the most beautiful ceremony in the world, but Sylvia wasn't going to protest.

"I forgot the question about if anyone has any good reason why these two people should not be married they are to speak up—" Deputy Wall looked out over the audience. "'Course it won't do any good since they were married last week and this is just an instant replay. But if you have anything to say, you might as well get it off your chest now."

There was a minute of silence. Someone coughed in the audience and, at a chastising glance from Deputy Wall, muffled it quickly.

"I know some of you think I should be the one speaking out against this whole marriage," Deputy Wall finally said. "And I'll have to admit that the angel—" he glanced down at Glory fondly "—and I have had our misunderstandings in the past, but that's all behind us. I'm here to say she's one of us now and I'd take a bullet for her. Just like I'd take a bullet

for any other citizen of the fine community of Dry
Creek, and I'd thank you to remember that come elec-
tion time this fall. I'd also—"

Mrs. Hargrove cleared her throat in warning.

Sylvia looked over at the older woman. She sat
with her arms crossed in the front pew of the church.
Next to Mrs. Hargrove, grinning throughout the ceremony, were Matthew's twin boys, Joey and Josh.
They had each carried a candle up to the altar earlier
in the ceremony and both Glory and Matthew had
bent down to kiss them before they began their vows.

"Anyway," Deputy Wall continued, "it's time for
the exchange of the rings. And since the rings have
already passed hands, so to speak, I want to present
the happy couple with another circle to remind them
of their meeting that took place right here in the fine
community of Dry Creek just several months ago."

Deputy Wall reached behind his belt and pulled off
the pair of handcuffs that were hooked there. He held
them up dramatically, giving the Billings reporter a
clear shot for a photograph. "These are the same
cuffs that I put around that hit man's hands when I
disarmed him right during our Christmas pageant—
saving Glory here from being shot and killed. For
their sentimental value, I'm giving them to Glory and
Matthew to remind them that they have friends in Dry
Creek—friends that would take a bullet for them. Not
that," he hurried to add, "we expect any more bullets
to be flying around—not with me on watch."

Deputy Wall gave the handcuffs to Glory with a
flourish. Sylvia was close enough to see that the handcuffs had been engraved with both Glory's and Mat-

thew's names and little hearts had been pressed into the metal. As she saw the reporter take his third photograph of the handcuffs, Sylvia had to admit that Deputy Wall knew how to stage publicity.

"And—for the record—no tax money was paid out for the cuffs."

Mrs. Hargrove cleared her throat again and, this time looked meaningfully at her watch.

"Well, it's getting time for dinner. And since the 'I do's' have already been said, and I expect put into practice—" Deputy Wall winked at Matthew "—I call this wedding official. I now pronounce you Mr. and Mrs. Curtis."

Glory and Matthew turned around and faced the people of Dry Creek.

Sylvia had no trouble looking at Glory now. Her friend's face was pink with happiness. Glory looked up at Matthew, and the love shining in her eyes warmed Sylvia until she felt tears in her own eyes. *Thank you, Lord, for this blessing for my friend.*

"Oh, I forgot—" Deputy Wall called out over the cheering. "He's supposed to kiss the bride."

Matthew wrapped his arm around Glory and drew her to him in a vigorous kiss that left no doubt of his affection. Sylvia felt more tears gather in her eyes. The love between Glory and Matthew was a beautiful thing to behold.

Garth patted his tuxedo, looking for a pocket. That was the trouble with fancy clothes—they never had any pockets, he thought to himself. And how was a gentleman to reach into his pocket and offer a lady a handkerchief, if he had no pocket? Garth was almost going to go looking for a handkerchief when Mrs. Hargrove stepped up to Sylvia.

"Here, dear," the older woman said, pulling a white lacy handkerchief out of her coat pocket and giving it to Sylvia. "Weddings always make me cry, too."

Garth grimaced. It was a sad day when he was outgentlemanned by Mrs. Hargrove.

Sylvia absentmindedly licked the butter off her fingertips and then remembered where she was and looked around quickly to see that none of the kids had seen her. Mrs. Buckwalter had given them a demonstration back in the kitchen on the correct way to eat a lobster, and it hadn't included any finger licking. Mrs. Buckwalter had been most emphatic about the use of the white linen napkins at each place setting.

Not that the people here would care who became impatient with napkins.

The whole town of Dry Creek had crowded into the café for the lobster dinner, and the quiet clatter of silverware could barely be heard over the laughing conversation of the people gathered. The café was so full that some of the ranch hands had taken their plates out to sit on the porch.

Mrs. Buckwalter had outdone herself. She'd had Jenny cook fresh asparagus and new potatoes to go with the lobster—although where she'd gotten the asparagus in February, Sylvia was afraid to ask.

"You know this isn't bad," one of the girls, Sarah, said quietly as she pulled some meat out of her cracked lobster. "I thought it'd taste funny, but it doesn't. It's all right."

"Just tastes like butter," Francis agreed as she dipped a chunk of lobster meat into a bowl of melted butter. "I haven't had lobster for years. I'd forgotten how nice it can be."

Sylvia noted that Garth had stationed two of the steadier ranch hands on either side of Francis at the table. They were quiet, muscular men who periodically checked the door. Garth wasn't taking any chances.

Francis, herself, seemed oblivious to the fuss. She was dressed in a long ruby-colored dress. The bottom floated around her like she was a Roman goddess while the top of her dress was covered with a practical, no-nonsense black wool jacket. It was a little chilly in the café.

"More lobster," Robert Buckwalter said as he pushed a utility cart close to the table where they sat. "It's freshly boiled. Ready for cracking."

Sylvia had to give Robert credit. For a rich man, he was a remarkably good sport. He had offered to help Jenny cook the lobsters and she'd said he'd make a better waiter than a cook so he'd gone to his plane and pulled out a tux. He looked every inch a sophisticated waiter.

"We don't usually eat lobster," Sylvia hastened to assure him. She didn't want him to think that the foundation's money was being used to feed her kids gourmet meals. "We've stuck more to the basics for meals."

Robert grimaced. "My mother told me. I wouldn't

call macaroni and cheese a basic. I just hope the news media never hears about it. They'd love to tear apart the Buckwalter Foundation for taking a bunch of city kids out to the country and giving them a major case of malnutrition.''

''We had carrots, too.''

''Well, that's something,'' Robert said glumly as he sat down in a metal folding chair next to Sylvia. The chair was scratched and it creaked when he settled back into it, but he didn't seem to care.

All of a sudden Sylvia noticed that Robert, even in his tux, was looking a little wilted. ''Tired?''

''I can't be,'' Robert said stiffly. ''I work out an hour every day in the gym. I do power exercises. Strength training. I'm in top physical shape. I could run a marathon. Pushing a few lobster around on a cart is nothing for me.''

''Good.''

Robert was silent for a moment. ''She doesn't like me, you know.''

Sylvia wiped the butter off her fingers and patted Robert's arm. ''Your mother?''

''My mother? Why would you think my mother doesn't like me?'' Robert turned and looked at Sylvia indignantly. ''Of course my mother likes me. It's her.'' Robert jerked his head toward the kitchen. ''She doesn't like me.''

''Ahh,'' Sylvia said in what she hoped conveyed sympathy. ''Jenny.''

''I offered to buy her an evening gown for tonight. Something special. I could have had a designer original here in three hours, maybe two,'' he boasted, snapping his fingers. Then he looked back down at the table. "She didn't want it. Wouldn't even talk about it. Said if I brought it here, she'd give it away to one of the girls."

"Maybe she had something else she wanted to wear," Sylvia offered.

Robert snorted. "She's wearing her chef's apron. Lobster stains and all. I think she's even going to wear that ridiculous hair net." Robert looked directly at Sylvia. "You're a woman. Tell me why any woman would turn down an evening gown—a designer original evening gown—in favor of an old chef's apron?"

Sylvia shrugged. "Why don't you ask her?"

"Maybe I will." Robert stood and started to push his cart back toward the kitchen.

"And ask her to dance while you're at it," Sylvia called after him.

Robert turned and nodded curtly. "I think I will."

Sylvia smiled to herself. The dance coming up was going to prove interesting.

Garth was watching Sylvia smile. She was standing in the middle of the barn and looking around at the decorations the kids had made this afternoon. There were long streamers of pink crepe paper and wedding bells from every rafter. The kids had actually made the old barn glitter. As Sylvia completed turning around and studying the decorations from every angle, her smile deepened until she glowed.

Now this, Garth said to himself, this is the Sylvia he wanted to dip on the dance floor. He looked around. Where was the music? The sooner he got to dancing, the sooner he could get to dipping.

Garth looked over Sylvia's shoulder. Good, Francis was sitting down with some of the older women in the town. He needed to keep her in sight. Not that there was much to worry about tonight as long as Francis stayed with the crowd of townspeople.

The quiet sound of music grew in volume until the rich sounds of a slow-dancing song filled the barn. Garth looked over—the sound system he had bought for the town when they hosted the Christmas pageant was being put to good use. He hoped they had a whole stack of slow cassettes. He didn't want to be moving too fast when he dipped Sylvia.

Sylvia needed to clear her throat. No, she needed to swallow. She wasn't sure what she needed to do. All she knew was that her throat had turned to cotton about two minutes into the dance with Garth. She felt as if she was thirteen again. She didn't even know where to put her hands. What she did know was that he was too close.

"Remember you're the leader," Sylvia finally mumbled into his shoulder.

Garth blinked. He was so caught up in the soft sway of the music and the smell of Sylvia's hair that he hadn't been paying attention.

"I'm sorry. Did I miss a step?"

Sylvia lifted her head and whispered distinctly, "I didn't say you're leading. I said you're the leader— the boys will be watching you."

Garth looked around. It didn't appear that the boys

were watching much except the girls they had in their arms. He looked back at Sylvia. "Why would they watch me?"

"They'll want to know how close they can dance with the girls."

Garth noticed that Sylvia had bright red spots on her cheeks. Her arms were braced against him, whether to hold him away from her or hold herself away from him he wasn't sure. "Isn't that up to the girls?"

"Of course not," Sylvia said shortly. "Teenagers need to know the limits and it's up to the adults to set them."

Garth looked around at the dancers again. "I don't see anyone who's dancing so close as to make it a problem."

"Well, they will be," Sylvia retorted softly. She half stumbled and Garth steadied her. "We need to be a good example."

Garth opened up his arms and gave Sylvia more room. "If you need more space, you can tell me. It doesn't need to be about the kids. It can be for you."

"I don't—I—" Sylvia sputtered and then took a breath and said simply, "Thank you."

"It's all right," Garth murmured as he slowed his step.

"I'm sorry." Sylvia removed her arms from Garth's shoulders and wrapped them around herself. "Maybe you want to dance with someone else. I—"

Sylvia looked up at him and Garth would have traded his ranch for the chance to pull her into his arms and comfort her. But it was clear she wouldn't be comforted by that gesture. She looked thoroughly miserable and nervous at the same time.

"I'm sorry," Sylvia repeated, and stared over Garth's shoulder. "I think maybe I'll go sit with the women. If you want to ask someone else to finish the dance, I'd understand."

"I don't need to finish the dance. I'm happy to sit out the rest of the night with you if that's what you want."

"But you won't get to show off your dip," Sylvia protested halfheartedly. "That's what you came for."

"I came to be with you," Garth corrected her softly. "I don't care about the dip."

"I'm sorry I'm not very entertaining tonight," Sylvia said as she started to walk toward the knot of older women who were sitting beside the door.

"You don't need to entertain me." Garth followed her. "I'm your friend. Friends sit with friends when they need them."

"I don't need anyone," Sylvia protested stiffly as she nodded a greeting to Mrs. Hargrove and sat down on a metal folding chair near the older woman. "I do just fine alone."

"Well, maybe *I* don't do so good when you're alone," Garth said in exasperation as he turned an empty metal chair around so that he could straddle it and sit facing Sylvia. "Maybe this is all selfish on my part."

"You're just being kind," Sylvia said woodenly as she rubbed her arms to warm them.

"No, I'm not being kind." Garth looked over at

Mrs. Hargrove. "Those heaters are working, aren't they? Sylvia's cold."

"You don't need to—"

"See that the heaters are working?" Garth finished for her in astonishment. "Can't a man do anything to help you without you pretending you're all right?"

"I am all right." Sylvia stopped rubbing her arms and smiled up at him brightly. "There, see. I'm fine."

Garth looked at Sylvia skeptically. The gown she wore was cut so low off her shoulders that he knew the skin of her back was pressed against the cold metal of the folding chair she was sitting in. Her arms were covered with goose bumps. Granted, the sight of her in that dress made his blood boil, but it didn't keep her warm. "I'll check the heaters."

"But—"

"If you're cold, other people will be, too," Garth insisted as he stood.

It was then that he noticed Mrs. Hargrove had stopped talking with Doris June who was sitting on her left side and was now looking to her right side and studying him and Sylvia with frank approval.

"Excuse me," Mrs. Hargrove said when she saw that she'd gained Garth's attention. "I couldn't help overhear. If Sylvia is cold, she's welcome to borrow Francis's jacket. Francis got up to dance and left it here. I'm sure she won't mind."

Mrs. Hargrove held up the black jacket that Francis had worn earlier. "Those old varsity school jackets— I see more of them around Dry Creek than you'd think. Before the old high school closed." She turned the jacket so Sylvia could see the emblem of the tiger on the back of it. "They were the fighting tigers. They were a small school, but they had pride."

"Who was Francis dancing with?" Garth asked, his eyes skimming the couples on the dance floor.

"Jess asked her."

Garth searched the dance floor again. "I don't see them." He looked at the people lining the walls of the barn, talking. "Are you sure she's not with someone else?"

"Why, no, it was Jess. Why, there he is himself—ask him."

Garth turned to the older man. "Is Francis with you?"

The older man flushed. "That's what I came to tell you. I excused myself to visit the men's room and when I came back, one of the kids said Francis went to the bus to get some cassette she'd brought. She said she'd be right back, but I looked and I didn't see her."

"She can't be gone." Garth said the words without thinking. He scarcely noticed that Sylvia had stood and put her hand on his arm.

"We'll find her." Sylvia comforted him. "She's probably just gone to the rest room. Or maybe she stopped to talk to someone. There's so many people here. She can't be far."

"I'll just go to the bus and check if the cassette is still there." Garth felt the emotion drain from him. He couldn't afford to feel anything. He needed to think. "Did she say what the song was?"

"'Blue Velvet.'" Jess shuffled his feet and looked

miserable. "I can ask around inside and see if she's talked to anyone."

Garth nodded. "I'd appreciate that."

"And I'll go with you," Sylvia offered decisively.

"You can't—we don't know who's out there."

"Whoever they are, they're not looking for me," Sylvia protested reasonably. "Besides, four eyes are better than two."

"Okay." Garth nodded. "She's probably just out looking at the stars anyway. She always did like the night sky."

Sylvia nodded and started to the door. "We'll find her."

"Wait," Mrs. Hargrove called. She held out the jacket to Sylvia. "You'll catch your death of a cold out there. Take this."

Sylvia walked back and took the jacket.

"Thanks," she said as she slipped her arms into the jacket sleeves and took the red knit scarf out of the pocket and wound it around her neck. "We'll be back soon."

Meanwhile, outside in the dark of night

Flint swore. No wonder being a hero had gone out of style. His leg still stung where Francis had kicked him in her glittery high-heel shoes, and one of his toes could well be broken where she had stomped on it. Next time he'd let the kidnappers have her. She was more than a match for most of the hired toughs he'd seen in his time.

And thinking of his toes, what was she doing with

shoes like that anyway? Women only wore shoes like that to please a man. She must have a boyfriend inside that old barn.

Flint's only consolation was that his horse seemed to know he needed her and was behaving for once.

"Now I know why I call you Honey," Flint murmured encouragingly as he nudged his horse down the dark road.

"Haaargh," the angry growl came from the bundle behind him, but Flint didn't even look back. Except for being temporarily gagged, Francis was doing better than he was. He'd even put his jacket around her. Not that she had thanked him for it.

"Yes, sir, you're a sweetie, all right." Flint continued quietly guiding his horse. Honey knew the way back to her home even if it was only a humble abandoned shed. That horse could teach some people the meaning of gratitude.

Or, if not gratitude, at least cooperation, Flint fumed.

If it wasn't for his years of training as an agent, Flint would have turned around and told Francis a thing or two. What did she think?

There was no time for the niceties after he heard those two hired thugs repeating their instructions about kidnapping Garth's sister in her black lion jacket. They planned to wait for her by the bus parked right next to that old cattle truck they'd come in. And they mentioned a third man would be coming to help. Flint had already identified the truck and disabled it as best he could by dumping some of the sand from the café's large ash can into the gas tank while the men were eating lobsters with everyone else. He'd cringed at having to do it, but the men had chained the hood shut so he couldn't get to the spark plugs. He would have disabled the three men, too, but Francis didn't have sense enough to stay inside long enough for him to do it.

He was halfway to the bus when he recognized her silhouette in the door as she opened it briefly. There was no time for fancy plans. The only way to protect Francis was to grab her first and worry about the men later.

He knew the men would be a problem, but he hadn't counted on Francis's resistance. He thought once she knew it was him she'd come quietly. Perhaps even gratefully. But the moment he saw recognition dawn, she fought him like he was out to kill her. He hadn't planned on gagging her until she made it clear she was going to scream.

And all the while she was kicking and spitting, he'd been doing her a great service.

Yes, he sighed, he could see why being a hero had gone completely out of style. It wasn't easy being the knight on the shining white horse. Not with women today. Come to think of it, it wasn't even easy with the horses of today. Honey made it clear she'd rather be eating oats than rescuing a damsel in distress.

"Tired. That's what you are," Flint said softly as he leaned over the horse's neck. Honey sighed and he gave the horse another encouraging nudge. "We're both tired, aren't we? But don't worry. We're almost there. Then I'll have something sweet for you."

The bundle behind him gave an indignant gasp and then another angry growl.

"I was talking to the horse." Flint smiled in spite of himself.

Chapter Twelve

Sylvia put her hands in the pockets of Francis's jacket. The ground in front of the barn was frozen and crusted with patches of old snow. The snow and dead grass crunched beneath her feet as she walked beside Garth. It must have been about ten o'clock and the night darkness was just turning deep. If it wasn't for the light streaming out of the barn doorway behind them, there would be no light except the distant stars in the sky.

"She has to be still here," Sylvia finally realized. "It's so dark we would see taillights from a car for miles. No one could have kidnapped her and already gotten away."

Garth grunted. "Unless he turned off his lights."

"In terrain like this?" Sylvia asked incredulously. "There are snowdrifts all along the road. And ditches on the side that you can barely see with lights. No one is that foolish."

"We can hope not," Garth said grimly. He privately thought that someone foolish enough to kidnap Francis wouldn't have sense enough to avoid getting stuck in a snowdrift.

"There's the bus." Sylvia saw the dark form of the bus emerge from the black night. It was still parked where they'd left it, next to the café. There were a few scattered pickups and one cattle truck next to it that must have been left by ranchers who had come in for the wedding reception. "All these outfits— that's probably why Jess couldn't see Francis. She's probably in the bus now looking for her cassette. Maybe it fell down beneath a seat."

"I don't see anyone in the bus." Garth worried as they walked closer.

Sylvia looked carefully. If Francis had gone inside the bus, wouldn't the door be half-open? And there were no dark shadows that looked like someone was inside walking down the bus aisle looking for something.

"You stay here," Garth ordered as he opened the bus door.

Sylvia hunched her shoulders. The jacket she'd borrowed was a little large and it left a gap that allowed air to funnel down her back. If she hunched her shoulders, she could close the gap. She could see a dark shadow of Garth as he walked down the bus aisle, checking in each of the seats. Maybe Francis was inside the barn still, Sylvia thought. Maybe she was having a good time and had just forgotten Garth would be worried if he didn't know where she was. *Please, Lord, protect her wherever she is.*

Sylvia could see the shadow of Garth as he turned and was now walking back down the aisle. She then suddenly smelled something. Her first thought was that it was an old rag that someone had left outside. It smelled of old garlic and sweat. Then she realized with a start that a rag left outside in the cold for any length of time would freeze and not smell at all. She didn't even have time to turn around before the rag was being passed over her eyes and down to her mouth.

"Aaarrrgh." Sylvia's scream was muffled as the rag settled into her mouth.

"Zahat taaa mugft." Sylvia tried to ask what had happened, but the words never left her mouth. She jabbed her elbows back, hoping to stop her attacker. But all she managed to jab was air. She was being captured by bulky shadows. She'd swear the men had not been there two seconds ago, and now they hovered over her. She couldn't see any faces, but she could smell the men. They smelled like old socks that had been worn hard and then tossed inside a gym locker to ripen.

"That's the jacket," one of the men said confidently to the other as he held Sylvia's hands behind her back. "It was easier than I thought. She didn't even give us much of a fight."

Sylvia tried to move at that one. She tried to tell them that the only reason she hadn't given them more of a fight was because she hadn't known they were coming. If they had fought fair, she would have gotten her licks in.

"Hmph," the other man said as he twisted a rope

around Sylvia's hands until she was securely bound. "Maybe she's just smart. Knows we wouldn't mind plugging her if she gave us any trouble."

Sylvia stilled herself. She needed to focus—and to see. She could barely see the detail in the men's clothing, but she knew she needed to locate the bulges that would tell her if the men were just trying to scare her or if they really had guns. If they were armed, she had to act fast. Garth was inside the bus and would be an easy target when he opened the bus door and stepped down.

Sylvia looked down. She wished there was something to kick. A bucket would make a big enough noise to alert Garth. But there was no bucket. The dirt ground was covered with patches of snow. There weren't even any rocks she could kick up against the side of the bus.

The only thing on the ground in front of her eyes were the four feet of the men holding her. Sometimes God calls us to be resourceful, she reminded herself, as she did what she had to do. She lifted her foot and stomped down hard on the toe nearest her.

"Hey, watch what you're doing!" the man protested loudly as he danced his feet back out of her reach.

"Shhh." The larger of the two men turned to the other and shushed him with a whisper. "Stop your caterwauling."

The man defended himself. "She pounded my toes."

"Forget about your toes. You can buy new toes

with what we'll get off this deal," the larger man ordered.

"Just make sure you tie her feet together before we take her to the boss," the injured man said. "He won't like something like that—might even decide it's our fault for not teaching her better manners while she was with us."

The injured man turned to Sylvia and smiled. Or, at least, she thought he smiled. She saw the white of his teeth as he bared them. And then she smelled the sour garlic. She'd seen friendlier smiles on the faces of the cougars at the Seattle zoo just before feeding time.

"Bet I could teach her some pretty manners," the man continued. "Pretty little thing like that. Would be a pleasure."

His voice was greasy with what Sylvia supposed served him as charm. It made her want to spray the air around her with disinfectant.

"We haven't got time for that nonsense," the larger man whispered wearily, and jerked his head to the barn. "You're forgetting we have an army over there who could come tramping out here. We need to get her out of here. The boss will know what to do with her."

Sylvia felt her blood turn cold. She didn't want to meet this boss. She wished they'd take the gag off so she could tell them they had made a mistake. The boss didn't want her. Then she realized her dilemma. They must want Francis, and if she told them that she wasn't Francis, they would go out and find the other woman instead. *Dear Lord, what do I do?*

* * *

Garth shifted his legs. He'd crouched down in the stairwell of the bus. The frost covered most of the window, but it had left a thin strip at the top. It was this strip that allowed Garth to see outside.

He'd counted two men, but he knew there was at least one more. He could tell from their murmured voices that they were only hired help. That meant there would be another man around. Hired help never worked without a lookout. That's part of what made them so successful. They didn't care enough to take unnecessary risks.

Garth felt around on the rubber mat behind him. When the bus driver had flown back to Seattle, he had left a long flashlight there. It was the closest thing to a weapon Garth could find. At first he picked it up and hefted it like a club. It wasn't heavy enough to do much damage. Then he had an idea and shifted the flashlight to its regular position.

Garth took a deep breath and pushed on the bus doors so they opened with a decisive swish. He counted on the sound of the doors opening to get the men's attention. It worked. The men both turned and looked straight at him. Then Garth raised the flashlight and clicked the button to the on position.

Good, thought Garth, the batteries were strong. The brightness spotlighted the two men and they froze, caught like deer in the headlights of an oncoming truck.

The light stopped the two men as no amount of hammering would have done. They had been out in the dark so long that night that the burst of light had to hurt their eyes.

"What the—?" one of the men said as he raised his hands to cover his eyes.

Garth didn't wait for a formal invitation. He tackled the man in his midsection while taking care to push the man he was aiming for into the other man. Garth had been up against two men a time or two in his life and he knew how to fight them. The key was to keep the action fast and always be a moving target. Most men, who were fighting more than one man, made the mistake of focusing. In a brawl one couldn't focus and win. One had to spin more than aim. And always remember the domino effect. A man pushed into another man makes both men fall.

Garth had the situation under control. He had one man in a hammerlock, the man's head in an elbow vise, while the other man lie moaning on the ground. Sylvia, a gag in her mouth and her hands tied behind her back, was squirming around and obviously trying to yell. Garth supposed she was doing what she could to help him by cheering him on, and the thought warmed him. Dancing wasn't the only way to win a lady's heart.

Garth was almost going to smile a victory smile at Sylvia when he felt it—a cold, little round circle pressed into the middle of his back.

"That's enough," the man's voice behind him said. "Be a pity to put a bullet hole in that fancy suit you're wearing. Rented, I expect. Still, they'd make your kin pay for it."

Garth carefully released his hold on the man in the hammerlock and the man fell to his knees. Garth thought carefully. He didn't want them to think he was poor just in case it made a difference. "The suit's mine." At least for tonight. He'd borrowed it from Robert Buckwalter. "From Italy."

The man with the gun whistled in respect.

Garth turned around slowly and checked on Sylvia. He couldn't read her eyes in the darkness, but he supposed she was frustrated with him. He hadn't gotten her message. Sylvia hadn't been cheering him on at all. She'd been trying to warn him.

"Italy, huh? You must get around more than most folks in this forsaken place." The man with the gun looked casual. Even in the darkness Garth could see a gun in one of the man's hands and a length of rope in the other. "Don't figure there's much call for suits when you spend your days slopping the hogs."

"This is cattle country," Garth said mildly as he looked away from Sylvia and focused on the man with the gun. The fact that the man was willing to talk was a good sign. It was always harder to shoot a man after a civil conversation with him. "Though we do have a few chickens. You ever raise a chicken?"

The armed man grunted and dipped his gun slightly to point at the man who was stirring at Garth's feet. "Lenny there used to have a dog. When we lived in Kansas. But that's the only animal we ever had. It died."

"Oh, you must be brothers, then?" Garth hoped the man would dip his gun again, this time farther down. A dip like that could be the only chance he'd get to disarm the man. "Never had a brother myself, but always thought it'd be good. Someone to get into scrapes with you.''

Garth kept his stance friendly. A hired killer would sense a tensed up body before Garth would get a chance to make his move. Garth willed his heart to slow down.

The man grunted and nodded his head toward Sylvia. ''Got yourself a sister, though. Bet you think a lot of her?''

Garth followed the man's eyes. So that was why they had Sylvia.

''Sometimes sisters can be a pain,'' Garth said casually. Before he claimed Sylvia as his sister, he needed to know if that fact would help her or harm her. He guessed it all depended on who was trying to take his sister. ''Once, mine up and ran off to Vegas and never even told me about it.''

The man with the gun looked completely indifferent.

Well, that eliminated Sylvia's ex-boyfriend as the gunman at least, Garth said to himself.

''Don't suppose the boss cares about that.'' Garth tried again. This illusive boss might be the ex-boyfriend, after all.

The gunman didn't answer that question. He seemed more interested in the other man behind Garth who was starting to stand. Garth knew that when the other man stood, his chances of getting the gun would be much less. Not that Garth needed to get the gun away from the man right away. If Garth could tease the man into firing the gun, the men inside the barn would know something was wrong.

"Come get the rope," the gunman ordered the man who was beginning to stand.

So that was why the man was so willing to chat, Garth thought. The man needed to wait for one of his buddies to recover enough to be able to tie the rope.

"Here." Garth turned slightly and spoke to the man behind him. "Let me give you a hand. It's Lenny, right?"

Garth held his breath while he began to pivot. Hopefully the man holding the gun would believe Garth was the old-fashioned, gentlemanly kind of man who would help his enemies, even when they were going to tie him up. Apparently the gunman did.

Garth was halfway turned when he made his move. He spun and fell to a crouch. The inevitable bullet from the man's gun buzzed quietly over his head. Garth's hopes fell. He hadn't seen the gun clearly, but he'd hoped it was just a plain unadorned gun. He'd counted on the sound of a gun shot to alert his men inside the barn that something was wrong. But the gun had a silencer on it. The quiet snapping sound it made wouldn't alert a gopher in a hole next to them.

Garth would have to do this the hard way. He rolled toward the gunman and, sensing more than seeing the man aim, quickly dodged to the side. The bullet slammed harmlessly into the frozen ground where Garth had been. Then Garth half rose and dove toward the man, tackling him at his knees. The man grunted in surprise. Garth rose up farther, knocking the gun out of the man's hand as he was struggling to aim it again.

The gun fell to the ground and Garth tried to kick

it under the bus. Instead it fell into a rut the tire tracks had made in the snow.

Sylvia tried to scream. She'd tried to scream ever since Garth had stepped out of that bus, but the gag choked back her screams and made her sound more like a cat in heat than a strong woman calling for help. Where was that deputy sheriff when they needed him?

It was unlikely anyone inside the barn would hear her scream or the scuffle by the bus. She wouldn't have even known bullets were being fired if she didn't hear the click of the gun and see the groove in the ground where the bullet buried itself.

Sylvia kept her eyes on Garth. He should have stayed in the bus. The other men hadn't known that anyone was inside the vehicle. She doubted very much they would have staged a search. There was nothing to be gained if both she and Garth were shot.

Sylvia strained to scream again.

Garth was breathing hard. He knew he should have kept up his army training exercises. He'd been able to do a hundred push-ups back then. These days he was lucky to squeeze out thirty. The three men were circling him like vultures waiting patiently for the final breath to leave their prey. Garth was obliging them by stepping around. Fancy dancing like a boxer did. Garth was hoping they wouldn't see the direction to his shuffling.

That gun was only four more feet away from him. Once he got close enough, he'd make a dive for it. He was beginning to hope it was the only gun in the game plan. None of the men had pulled out another weapon. They must be amateurs if they didn't come more prepared than that, but Garth didn't have time to waste worrying about whether they were hardened criminals or fools down on their luck enough to take a job like this.

Garth was only two feet from the gun now. Easy reaching distance. The men had closed in until they were about three feet from him. They still looked hesitant.

"He ain't all that much," Lenny finally muttered. "Don't know what the boss was so fussy about. Them Purple Hearts don't mean much when a man's old."

The man closest to Garth grunted. "He's no older than you are. Not so sure he couldn't take you and Buck both if you were here alone."

Garth took his breath silently. He was finally convinced Francis's ex-boyfriend wasn't behind this. Garth didn't get the Purple Hearts until he was back home, and Francis's boyfriend was gone by then. Garth had clung to the hope that it was this Flint. The alternative was chilling. Somehow that crime syndicate who was doing the rustling had found out he'd promised to help the FBI. They may have even found out that he'd already given the FBI one important clue and was soon to deliver another.

But what would they want with Francis?

Now, Garth muttered in his mind as he dove for the gun. The night was still dark and he was grateful for the black handle of the gun. Even in the shadows it stood out clearly from the white snow surrounding it.

Garth had guessed wrong. He realized that as he heard the angry grunts of the men above him and then the click of a trigger behind him. Just because the other two men hadn't pulled their guns earlier didn't mean they didn't have them.

The palm of Garth's hand pressed flat onto the frozen ground where the gun had been before one of the men kicked it away.

Garth had missed his chance. He quickly rolled away from the gun. He knew what was coming. The bullet slammed into the ground just inches from his side.

"What're you doing?" The man who had the silencer earlier hissed at someone over Garth's head.

Garth thought the man was talking to him until he heard the whine of the other man answering him. He rolled over and faced them.

"He was goin' for the gun," Lenny mumbled, jerking his gun at Garth again. "I ain't going to let him take a shot at me. Silencer or no silencer. Have to shoot him.."

"The boss still won't like it. Neither will the men inside that barn," the other man said. "They could've heard the bullet. I told you to get a silencer for that gun before we came out here."

Garth listened hopefully. The shot had not been loud since the ground had muffled it some. Lord knows he could still hear the shot ringing in his ear. But apparently no one inside the barn had heard it. If they had, he would be hearing the door on the barn open up and the people inside shouting, wondering what was wrong.

The night was silent as a tomb. The men had been lucky.

Apparently one of the men thought the same thing. "Get them into the back of the truck. We're getting out of here."

The man walked over to the back of the cattle truck that stood to the right of the bus.

Garth saw his chance. He could roll left under the bus and be into the café before the men could reach him. They likely wouldn't even be able to shoot him under the bus as the shadows were so deep. The only problem was Sylvia. He couldn't take her with him— not with her being so far away and having her hands tied. And he couldn't leave her.

Lenny grunted at Garth. "Don't try anything. I shot at you once. I'll do it again. Don't care what the boss says."

"Well, you better care." The other man scolded him impatiently as he hoisted himself up into the back of the truck to pull up the gate. "Don't be dim-witted. I explained how this job was different. Nobody messes with this kind of boss."

Garth's heart sank. It was the crime syndicate. They were in big trouble. He looked over at Sylvia. Even in the darkness he could see the tension in her body. She was frozen. She knew what the men were saying, too. And given her fear of violence, it must be painfully hard for her.

"Leave her here." Garth jerked his head toward Sylvia. "Take me if you have to, but leave her here. She doesn't know anything your boss wants to know anyway." Garth felt the sweat break out on his forehead. He needed to convince them. "She doesn't know a cow from a heifer. Or a Guernsey from a

Holstein.'' He saw the two men on the ground exchange worried glances. It was clear they didn't know, either. ''She'd only waste your boss's time. She wouldn't know a rustler if she met up with one in a dark alley. She'll only slow you down.''

''Just get your sorry face up there,'' the man with the gun finally ordered defiantly as he pointed to the back of the truck. ''We'll let the boss decide who knows what and who doesn't. Holstein, Guernsey or pure horse manure. We only deliver. It's up to him to sort it out.''

''Well, it's your funeral.'' Garth forced himself to be nonchalant as he drew his knees up and then stood. He casually brushed the snow off his suit. Anything to stall. Maybe someone had heard something and would think to check in a minute or two.

''Get in the truck,'' the gunman repeated impatiently.

''In a minute,'' Garth said as he continued brushing. ''The snow will ruin this suit if I don't get it off before it melts.''

Lenny snorted. ''Who cares? You ain't gonna need it where you're going.''

''Cost me six hundred dollars,'' Garth said with mock indignation as he continued brushing. ''Imported from Italy.''

''What's the holdup?'' the man inside the cattle truck called down to them.

''He needs to clean his suit,'' Lenny yelled back.

''What the——?'' The man inside the cattle truck stuck his head out of the back opening.

Lenny looked up and whined, "I might want that suit."

"You've never worn a suit in your life." The man inside the truck snorted. "No reason to start now. Just get them up here and make it snappy."

"I'll go a lot quicker if you leave her here." Garth stopped brushing his suit and laid his cards out on the table.

"Worried about your sister, huh?" The man standing inside the truck asked with a sneer. "Well, if you're really worried about her, you'll get your sorry butt up here or I'll—"

Garth felt his heart squeeze. The man standing on the truck had pointed the gun with the silencer straight at Sylvia.

Garth didn't take any chances. It took him five long strides to reach Sylvia. He didn't care if they shot him on the way there. He didn't breathe until he was standing in front of her. "There's no need to talk about shooting anyone. I'm cooperating."

"Good." The man on the truck bed grunted. "'Cause the boss didn't say nothing about keeping her alive. Now, you he's a little fussy about. But her—she's nobody, if you get my meaning."

Garth got his meaning. That was the reason they wanted his sister. They wanted some way to convince him to do whatever it was they wanted. "You tell that boss of yours that if he harms one hair on her head, he's bought himself more trouble than he can handle. He won't just answer to me—he'll answer to an even bigger boss."

"Who's that?" Lenny asked nervously.

"Someone who could grind your boss into chicken feed if he wanted." Garth hoped God didn't mind being referred to in those terms. And he hoped Sylvia was praying. He wasn't too sure God would answer his prayers. He and God had an understanding that Garth could look out for himself. But if Sylvia was praying, it'd be all right. The Almighty couldn't say no to Sylvia.

"You're sure we should—" Lenny asked his brother on the truck bed.

"Just get them up here," the man inside the truck ordered. "Don't you know a bluff when you hear one? I swear you're the dumbest of all us kids. You take after Uncle Joe."

"I do not—" Lenny protested indignantly, but he turned his attention to Garth and Sylvia. "Get on up." He gestured with his gun toward the truck bed.

Chapter Thirteen

Sylvia tried to concentrate on the openings between the wooden slats that made up the frame of the truck bed. She could barely see them. It was like seeing a black slat against the even deeper black of the night. She could feel where the slats were, easier than she could see them. The openings between the slats provided the only fresh air coming into the back of the truck and it came in small frigid streams. She lifted her head to align it with one of the slats. She needed the fresh air so she wouldn't pass out.

She'd never been so scared in her life.

She was frozen with fear and couldn't stop the trembling. She wondered what Garth thought. She was scooped inside of him and felt the tension all along his body. He was coiled and ready to spring. The men had tied them up together when they finally pushed them up into the back of the truck. Ordinarily, being tied up spoon-style with a man would make her heart race with fear. Maybe it still was—she couldn't tell. The other fear was so overwhelming, she couldn't separate which trembling came from which fear.

"I'd never hurt you," Garth pleaded softly in her ear. "You don't need to be afraid of being close to me. I'd never hurt you."

Sylvia realized Garth must have been whispering those words over and over into her ears. He was saying them like a chant.

Lord, he must think I'm a ninny. I'm not afraid of him.

It took a moment for the realization to sink even farther into her mind. She checked the nerves in her stomach. She shifted slightly to pull at the rope that tied her to Garth. Yes, she thought to herself in quiet jubilation, she was not scared of Garth. They were sitting here, thigh to thigh, torso to torso—tied up like two circus clowns in a barrel—and she, Sylvia Bannister, was not afraid.

Not that, she hesitated to assure herself, it had much to do with Garth himself. No, it must be that she had just never been forced to live with her fears long enough to conquer them before. She'd never had to sit inside a man's lap until the trembling stopped. That must be it.

It must be. Because the alternative—that she had special feelings for Garth that made her fears disappear, that maybe she was even a little bit in love with the man—was starting up a trembling all of its own. And this trembling rocked her to her foundations.

Dear Lord, I'm in a mess. What do I feel for him?

Garth wished he'd paid more attention when Matthew had explained prayer to him. On the long drive over to Seattle, they'd talked about everything. Even Matthew's ability—and at times, lack of ability—to pray.

Garth had never been fond of prayer. It always seemed somewhat sissy to him to have to ask anyone for help, even God. Not that Garth was opposed to other people praying. It seemed all right for them. In fact, he wholeheartedly supported it for some folks. But Garth had been raised to take care of himself, and prayer had never been part of his life.

His father had taught him that help was to be accepted warily as it always came with strings. A man didn't accept help unless he could pay it back in good measure and soon.

When he was alive, Garth's father was the king of bargainers. He figured everything was a deal made between two people and that the number-one rule was that only fools believe in free lunches. Everything had a price and the price needed to be checked out before the favor was accepted. If Garth's father had been around, the Trojan horse would still be rotting outside the village walls.

In short, the Elktons didn't trust the help of anyone, not even God.

What his father had never taught Garth was what to do when he needed help. Like now. His heart was breaking with love for this woman sitting here trembling in his lap and there was nothing he could do to make her trust him. He couldn't fight her ghosts. He hadn't been there in her past to protect her. He couldn't go back in time and change things.

He was helpless in the face of her fear. She was shaking like a leaf in his arms and he could do nothing. He couldn't even cuddle her as that would only make her more afraid.

No, Garth's father had never told him what to do when there was no one who could help him but God alone—not even when Garth needed that help more than he needed life itself.

Garth didn't even know how to talk to God. He just knew he needed to try.

Well, You know I'm not very good at this. Garth started to fumble a prayer. *Should have talked to You long before now. Wouldn't blame You if You decided not to help me. But if You have any mercy with my name on it, use it to get Sylvia out of here. She didn't ask for this. They can have my sorry hide. But not her. I refuse to let them have her.*

Garth stopped. He knew God had no reason to listen to him. Garth had never even pretended to listen to God. He had no way to pay God back. He knew of no way to prove his sincerity. No way to show how important this was to him. Unless—the thought came to him with the force of a sledgehammer. He didn't even stop to consider whether or not his father's rules would apply in this situation. He only hoped they did for he had one small thing he could offer God.

Lord, Garth continued. He felt the pain slice through him. *If you do this for me—get Sylvia out of here alive—I'll give up any claim to her. Not that I*

*have one. I've never been good enough for her. But
I'll lay down any hopes I have.*

There, Garth thought to himself, if God knew anything about him, He would have to know Garth was
sincere. He'd just offered all he could to repay the
favor. Not even God could ask for more.

Sylvia shifted. She was suddenly too warm. She
knew the temperature was freezing. But the direction
her thoughts were taking was heating her up like an
oven. She'd been tied in Garth's arms ever since one
of the three brothers had coaxed the sputtering engine
to life. The truck had run fine for a couple of miles,
but then the engine had started hammering away at
itself, making so much noise, Sylvia half hoped the
men in the barn could hear them if they stepped outside.

She was obviously not the only one who had noticed the engine.

"Thought you got that thing tuned up." Two of
the brothers—Buck and Lenny—were squatting down
in opposite corners at the front of the truck bed and
they were arguing quietly. Sylvia wondered if it was
any warmer closer to the cab. In the darkness she
could not see their faces, but she could see their
shapes. "We ain't even making five miles an hour.
For pity sakes, you was supposed to see to the tune-
up when we were in Miles City."

"I did."

"Does that sound like you got the truck tuned up?"
Buck demanded impatiently.

There was silence while the brothers listened to the
heavy chugging of the engine.

"But I did take it to that shop—remember the place was painted blue? Cost me eighty bucks."

Buck grunted again. "You got taken then. They might have took your money. But they didn't do nothing to that engine."

"I could go back—get my money back," the younger man offered softly.

"Why don't you just put in a complaint with the Better Business Bureau while you're at it?" Buck suggested sarcastically. "I swear, sometimes I think you're even stupider than Uncle Joe. You can't go back there. We've just kidnapped these two and who knows where that'll lead...."

Buck let his voice trail off and then he turned his attention to Sylvia and Garth. "You two been mighty quiet."

Sylvia blinked. In the darkness it was almost possible to pretend that the two men were just voices in the air. They were not real in the dark in the same way that Garth was. She felt his muscle around her. His warm breath on the top of her head. When the truck hit a bump in the road, it was Garth's legs that held her in place.

"Didn't know you required our conversation," Garth said quietly to the two men. "Sounded like you're doing pretty good on your own. You know, if it was me, I'd think some about that getting your money back on that tune-up. You can tell something's wrong. The truck acting up like this might be a sign."

One of the brothers grunted. "A sign of what?"

Garth kept his voice pitched low. He didn't want them to know how desperate he was for them to listen to him. He took a deep breath. The faint scent of peaches came to him along with the old scent of cattle. The peaches were from Sylvia. She had miraculously stopped trembling a little bit ago and had settled farther into his contours. He couldn't help himself. He used his forearms to try and cuddle her closer. If he didn't know better, he'd swear she'd snuggled into him.

"Could be a sign of trouble." Garth forced his mind back to the brothers. "Sometimes when something goes wrong right off in a mission, it's best to scrub the whole thing. Learned that with my buddies in the army. Once one thing goes wrong, it's downhill from there. Some good men died because they didn't listen to the signs."

"Do you think maybe—" Lenny began to whisper.

"I swear you have oatmeal for brains," the older brother scolded impatiently. "Don't you see what he's trying to do? He wants to psyche us out."

"Suit yourself," Garth said casually. He was glad the brothers couldn't see him in the darkness. He shifted his shoulder. He'd trade his left arm if he could move his right one to enclose Sylvia properly. What kind of demon had tied their hands together in front like this with his arms loped over Sylvia's shoulders? The most he could do was hug her neck.

"But what if—" Lenny whispered again, this time more quietly.

"We wouldn't even need to tell the boss you changed your mind," Garth offered. A strand of Sylvia's hair was flying free and ticking his cheek. He'd never felt anything softer. "Just take us back to the dance and we can pretend this never happened. I'll even take your truck back to my ranch and fix it properly so you can go home—wherever that is. The boss won't even know what happened."

Buck grunted. "The boss would know."

"Well, then we can talk to the deputy sheriff. Maybe he could arrest you—"

"What?" Buck protested indignantly.

"Hear me out," Garth continued. "If you take us back now, you won't do much time at all. Maybe just some probation or something. And if the boss is real big—" Garth already had a strong suspicion about who the boss was, and if Garth was right, the men were wise not to sell out too soon. "Well, if he's real big, you can turn state's evidence. Get put in the witness protection program. Get a whole new life somewhere—maybe Florida or someplace where it's real warm. They set you up with a cozy house. Three solid meals a day. A big-screen TV. Laying in the sun, sipping lemonade. Maybe get a dog for Lenny. Could be a great life."

"It *is* cold up here," Lenny dreamed quietly.

"We ain't turning no state's evidence," Buck said emphatically. "The Gaults aren't tattlers."

"But—" Lenny protested softly.

"No. Mama raised us better," Buck repeated firmly. "We took on the job and we'll finish it. No matter what we need to do when we get these two delivered to the boss."

Garth didn't argue further. Talk of what the brothers thought they might need to do stopped him. He'd known all along that the boss wouldn't want witnesses when he'd finished interviewing them. Still, he didn't want Sylvia to hear the words spoken.

The dark inside the back of the truck was so final that even the air smelled empty. The cattle truck had been built to keep cattle warm on cold winter drives. Its roof kept the stars from opening up the blackness of the night. On a summer night a deep darkness like this felt like velvet. But not in the biting cold of winter. The dark of this night reminded Garth of the suffocating lack of light found in deep caves that went so far down in the earth, there was no surface light left. Garth had been in a cave like that once. That kind of darkness chilled a man.

In the darkness of the truck bed, all was quiet except for the coughing of the truck engine and the distant rumble of— Garth listened closer. He'd swear that was the rumble of that Seattle bus pulling a load and pulling it hard.

Garth shifted his arm to try and communicate his excitement to Sylvia before he realized he needn't. Sylvia was clearly nervous and trying to communicate something to him through her gag. It sounded like boos, woos—no, boys.

Garth followed her thinking and felt a sinking feeling. Suddenly he hoped that it wasn't the bus he heard. Because if it was the bus, it meant that it must be the boys who were coming to their rescue. Jess was the only one of his hired hands who would drive the bus and he couldn't see well enough at night to take the wheel. Besides, adults would surely have had sense enough to send Deputy Wall and his siren instead.

Sylvia started to pray that the truck would go faster. She didn't want the boys to catch them. But the old truck was sputtering worse than ever. At this rate, the bus would catch them in seconds. And here she was, not even able to talk. Maybe if she could talk, she could explain about the boys. Lenny and Buck didn't seem such bad men. Not really. Maybe they'd let the boys off with a warning.

Garth felt Sylvia's neck move. She must be chewing at the gag in her mouth, trying to work it down. He knew from the angle that she didn't have much of a chance at it. She needed help. Garth could not see in the dark, so he moved his chin closer to the back of her head. Her hair was soft and smelled faintly of peaches. If they got out of this alive, he'd buy her a case of that shampoo she used. He'd never eat a fresh peach again without thinking of Sylvia.

Garth could feel Sylvia stiffen as he nuzzled her hair, trying to locate the knot.

"Easy," he soothed her, not daring to explain what he was trying to do in case Buck and Lenny were listening. He felt the rag tangled in her shoulder-length hair. Garth had never noticed the texture of hair as closely as now. He couldn't see her hair clearly. It was more shadows than anything. But the texture—it wasn't soft like a baby's hair. No, he could tell it belonged to a grown woman. Full-bodied and strong. He rubbed his chin more deeply into the waves of her hair and found the knot holding her gag in place.

Garth positioned his chin above the knot and tried to push downward on the rag. By now Sylvia must have figured out what he was doing because she'd become still. The rag was tight and didn't move.

Garth wasn't sure how much of this he could take. Nuzzling Sylvia's hair was reminding him too much of what he'd like to do if he was alone in the dark with her. He didn't suppose she'd notice if he— Garth brushed his lips lightly against the back of Sylvia's neck and held his breath. Good, she hadn't noticed. He knew because she hadn't pulled away from him or even tensed up.

His relief quickly turned to a dry taste in his mouth. A stolen kiss wasn't as sweet as he imagined it would be. It only reminded him of what a full-blown, real one would taste like—one that Sylvia didn't return, as well.

It was time for teeth, Garth decided. It was the only way he knew to get Sylvia's gag worked down far enough so that she could talk.

"Something's coming," Buck announced from the truck bed as he pounded on the back of the cab and shouted to the brother who was driving. "Get this thing moving."

Garth heard the truck driver trying to shift gears. Instead of shifting, the truck gave a belch and then a few feeble rumbles as it slowed to a crawl.

"I said, get it moving," Buck called frantically to his brother. "We got company."

The truck took a final cough and stalled completely.

There was a moment's silence in the dark truck bed.

Then Lenny whispered, "What're we gonna do now?"

"Get your gun ready," Buck said wearily. "If we can't outrun them, we have to outshoot them."

"But they're only children," Sylvia protested.

Garth congratulated himself. He'd moved the gag down enough for Sylvia to talk.

"Can't be helped," Buck said. Garth could hear the man stand to his feet. The scrape of his boot heels along the wood of the truck bed announced he had pulled himself up to a kneeling position and then a standing one.

"No need to shoot anyone," Garth reasoned calmly. "They can't stop you anyway. They're only kids. You still have the one your boss wants—me. I'm not planning on going anywhere, so just let Sylvia talk to the kids and order them back to the dance and—"

"How stupid do you think we are?" Lenny whined triumphantly. "Even I can see that's a trap. They go back and call the law, and before you know it we have more cops around here than flies."

"There are no flies in February around here," Garth continued, his voice pitched low and soothing. "And that's just how many cops you'd have to worry about. No, the smart thing is to let us tell the kids to go back home—let them take Sylvia with them. She knows you're serious. She'll be sure they do what you ask."

"I'm not leaving you here," Sylvia protested quietly.

"You'll do it for the kids." Garth felt prickles of

cold sweat on his shoulder blades. What did she mean, she wouldn't go? "We'll both do it for the kids. The boss only wants to talk to me. I can take care of myself."

For the first time in his life he said those words and followed them with a prayer. *Remember our deal. I'm counting on You. Keep Sylvia and the kids safe and You can have me.* He kept talking to be sure he sounded convincing to Sylvia. Everything depended on her being willing to leave. "No need to worry. I've been in tight places before and come out all right. Right now we need to think of the kids."

"But—" Sylvia began to protest when they heard the bus pull to a stop behind the truck.

Buck and Lenny had moved to the back of the truck and they were peering out between the slats.

"See anything?" Buck whispered to Lenny.

Garth could see the two black shadows at the end of the truck bed. He could also see the guns in their hands.

"Don't you know what hostages are for?" Garth finally demanded. He could hear the bus door opening slowly. That and what sounded like the muffled hoof-beats of a horse in the distance. "You take me and threaten to shoot me if anyone comes closer."

Garth didn't know how else to keep those kids in the bus. For all he knew, the kids didn't even know what they were up against. For all he knew they were out here to ride horseback in the moonlight and thought there were cows in this truck.

Garth saw the two shadows turn around.

"Think they'd do it?" Lenny whispered to Buck.

"Might be the kids don't like him all that well. He's kind of mouthy."

"The kids like me," Garth assured them. "The boys especially."

"I don't know—" Lenny wavered.

"For Pete's sake, they let me teach them to dance!"

"Did, huh?" Lenny said in surprise. "Guess they must, then."

"Hold it right there," Buck shouted from the truck. "We've got hostages and we'll start shooting them if you don't back off."

Buck shot a hole in the roof of the cattle truck for emphasis.

Garth squeezed his arms tight around Sylvia. She'd stopped trembling some time ago. He figured the shock had frozen her by now.

"No need to go shooting." Garth forced himself to continue to speak calmly. He firmly believed no one ever shot a man while they were talking. It was human nature to at least wait for the final sentence to be said.

"Yeah, we'll have to pay for that when we take the truck back," Lenny whined.

The sound of the hoofbeats came closer. Garth listened to see if the beat matched any of his horses. It didn't. Strange. Who else would have a horse out tonight?

"Everyone get back in the bus," Garth shouted. He decided to do the talking for the brothers. "Turn the bus around and go back to the dance."

The hoofbeats stopped. Whoever had been riding

up had reached the bus. Garth only hoped the horse was being ridden by someone with sense—which, come to think of it, didn't seem likely. Only a fool would be out riding a horse on a night as cold as this.

The hushed sound of Lenny and Buck whispering together made Garth uneasy before he heard the words from Buck. "I suppose it could be the boss out there. He must ride. And we are late in getting Elkton to him."

"No." Sylvia twisted in Garth's arm.

Garth felt the worry coil through her.

"Best not be shooting out there, if the boss is there," Garth said, as much for Sylvia's benefit as he did for the brothers'. "Wouldn't want to make any mistakes in the dark. 'Course, don't suppose it'd be so bad if you shot the man dead—but I wouldn't want to be in your shoes if you only wounded him."

Garth hoped the brothers were wrong. The rhythm of the hoofbeats suggested the horse was well past its prime. Maybe it wasn't the boss out there with those kids.

Lenny and Buck looked at each other. Garth could almost hear them thinking.

"Boss? That you?" Buck finally called out.

There was silence. Garth was almost ready to feel relief.

"The boss sent me," a man's deep voice finally answered. "Told me to tell you to call it off. He's changed his mind."

Lenny and Buck whispered together.

"How do we know the boss sent you?" Buck called back. "He'll have our hides if we don't—"

"Shhh—" Lenny's frantic whisper interrupted Buck and led to another huddled conversation.

"I was just up the canyon," the man's voice continued smoothly. "The boss was sitting out there in his Ford pickup chomping on some chewing tobacco. You know how he likes his chewing tobacco. Now, what was the brand name he uses...?"

Buck and Lenny had stopped whispering midway through the man's words.

"Black Medicine," Lenny said quietly to Buck. "He chews Black Medicine. I saw the can when we were up there talking. He reached into his pocket and pulled it out—"

Garth let out his breath. He didn't know he'd even been holding it until he felt his whole body relax.

"The boss must have changed his mind," Garth repeated for the brother's benefit.

Garth decided he'd seen a miracle. Only God could have pulled this one off.

The relief that flooded Garth was followed by a gut punch. If God had done what Garth had asked, that meant Garth had to do what he promised. Just let Sylvia sit in my lap a little longer, he bargained—just a little longer. Forever will be a long time without her.

Sylvia rubbed her wrists. The brothers had taken the bait whole. They'd stepped down from the truck and into the arms of first one and then two lawmen. The weak lights from the bus showed the three brothers bound and gagged in the middle of the frozen road. The kids had had the presence of mind to bring along Deputy Wall, and then there was a federal agent. Who would have thought a federal agent would be out riding horseback just when they needed one? Granted, he didn't look too happy to be there. Sylvia would guess he hadn't slept in three or four days and he kept muttering something about women, but she didn't care. He was a miracle.

Yes, she thought to herself in satisfaction, tonight was a night for miracles. She could hardly wait to show Garth that she was no longer afraid of him. He might assume from her lack of fear that she'd fallen in love with him, but she decided to tell him anyway. Maybe she was a little in love with him. Her friend Glory had been telling her all along that Garth was just waiting for her to come around. Well, tonight was a night for miracles.

"I'm glad you were with me in there," Sylvia said shyly, walking over to where Garth stood. She hadn't made a move on a man in years. If it wasn't Garth that she was talking to, she wouldn't have had the nerve. "I felt safe with you there."

Now if that isn't a road map to my feelings, nothing is, Sylvia thought to herself in quiet satisfaction.

"No problem," Garth said quietly, and then moved over to where the boys were standing by the open bus door.

Sylvia couldn't move. She didn't know what she had expected. But she hadn't expected him to treat her announcement so coldly. He hadn't even looked at her, let alone smiled. He'd been smiling at her like a model in a toothpaste ad ever since he showed up in Seattle, and now, when she wanted nothing more than to see a smile, he just turned away.

It's too late, she thought to herself bleakly. Or maybe I was wrong. He sure didn't look the least bit interested. Maybe I misread his friendliness. She looked at him again, standing over by the boys. She'd forgotten about the boys. His friendliness must have only been a tool to guide the boys in the art of being gentlemen.

She lifted her chin in pride. Well, she could get along without him in her life. She could get along just fine without him.

Chapter Fourteen

Garth was chopping wood.

He'd been chopping wood for three days now and had just sent a couple of his hired hands over to Augusta to bring back another truckload of the waste timber the forestry service had for sale. He had steadfastly refused to use the electric saw even though he had blisters on both of his hands from the heft of the ax. Jess had carefully placed the saw within easy reaching distance two days ago and then had hung around watching him, shaking his head and muttering that they had gas heat anyway so who needed all that wood.

Garth didn't stop to explain that he wasn't chopping the wood because he needed wood. He was chopping the wood because he needed to chop. He needed the satisfying crack as he buried the ax blade deep into the wood.

"Want some coffee?"

Garth was prepared to scowl at whoever was interrupting him until he looked up and saw that it was Matthew. Matthew was standing beside the mountain of wood Garth had chopped and was holding two mugs of coffee in his hands.

"As I remember, you take it black," Matthew said as he held out one of the mugs toward Garth. "You didn't answer my call so thought I'd come in person."

Garth took one last swing and drove the ax blade into the trunk of what had been a diseased tree. "Been busy."

The only call Garth had taken in the past three days was one from his contact at the FBI telling him that the crime syndicate behind the beef rustling was falling apart. The Gault brothers had known enough to finger "the boss" and he was on the run to Mexico. The FBI didn't think there would be any further trouble in Montana.

"Mrs. Hargrove tells me that agent that showed up is Francis's old boyfriend," Matthew said as he settled himself on top of a pile of kindling. "Thought it might be worrying you."

Garth looked over at the man he'd come to know as his friend on their long drive over to Seattle several weeks ago. "Not a bit. Francis told me it was none of my business and I believe her. She's a grown woman. If they want to let the past stay the past, who am I to question it? It was a bit of a shock, but I'm fine with it."

"So that's not what's worrying you?" Matthew repeated thoughtfully.

"What makes you so certain something's worrying me?" Garth asked indignantly.

Matthew cocked his head at the stack of chopped wood.

"Can't a man chop a little wood without somebody thinking something's wrong?"

"Well, it's not exactly a little wood," Matthew said ruefully. "And you do heat with gas. According to Jess, you'll both be long gone before you use up all that wood."

"Tell Jess to speak for himself. I intend to—to build some fires in my fireplace," Garth said staunchly and then winced. Watching a fire all alone sure sounded like a desolate way to spend a winter evening. He supposed, though, he might as well get used to it. His whole life stretched before him—more empty and barren than he would have ever imagined possible before he met Sylvia.

"I see." Matthew took a sip of his coffee and settled more comfortably into the woodpile. "I didn't figure there was anything wrong. After all, if I've ever seen a man who had it all made, it'd have to be you."

Garth grunted. "Yeah."

"You've got a good piece of property."

"The best."

"And a sister who thinks a lot of you."

Garth grunted again. Matthew was right. He did have a lot to be thankful for.

"Yes, sir, God has blessed you big-time."

"God can mind his own blasted business from now on." Garth put down his mug of coffee and started to rise.

"Ahhh." Matthew took another sip of his hot coffee. "So it's God you're mad at?"

"I'm not mad at anyone," Garth said as he walked toward the ax and hefted it. He raised it and aimed it square at the heart of a twisted tree limb. "Got no reason to be mad. God and I understand each other."

"That so?"

"Yes," Garth said as he swung the ax and hit the tree limb, shattering it in two. "We've got an understanding."

"Just out of curiosity, what would that understanding be?"

Garth eyed the other man warily. "You asking as my minister?"

"Didn't know you've been going to church enough lately to see me as your minister."

"I've thought about going. Been thinking about it for months. Almost drove down for a service last month."

"Ahhh." Matthew nodded and set his coffee down. "Well, then I guess I could answer as your minister if that's what you want."

"Don't have much use for ministers." Garth twisted the ax handle, breaking another piece off the tree limb.

"Yeah, we can be a frustrating lot," Matthew agreed mildly as he lifted his coffee cup and took a sip.

"No offense."

"None taken."

"It's just all this deal making," Garth finally said as he took the pieces of tree he'd cut and threw them on top of the huge woodpile. "Something's not right when God holds all the cards."

"God doesn't hold all the cards. We have free will."

"Some free will—it doesn't help us much in tight situations."

"Like when you were kidnapped? But God got you out of there. John had gone outside and just happened to see them putting you in the back of the truck. I have to believe God had a hand in the timing of that."

Garth looked over at the other man. Confusion was stamped on Matthew's face.

"I know God got us out of there—believe me, I know. I prayed for Him to do it and He answered my prayer."

"Well, that's good, isn't it?"

"Yeah." Garth sighed, dug his ax blade into another tree limb, then sat down next to Matthew. "I'm glad He answered my prayer— He kept the kids and Sylvia safe. I owe Him everything for that. And that's what I promised to give Him so I've got no complaints. I aim to pay up on my debt. We Elktons stand by our word."

"I don't suppose there's any chance that what you promised to give God was your love, devotion and a life of service to Him?"

Garth looked at the minister as if the man had gone balmy. "What would He want with me? No, I gave Him the only thing I figured He'd want—I promised to stay away from a certain woman whom I know He regards very highly."

Matthew chuckled as though he finally understood. "Sylvia."

"I'm not naming any names."

"You don't have to name names." Matthew smiled widely. "You're forgetting I drove to Seattle with you. I had to listen to you rehearse your 'I'm in the neighborhood, thought I'd drop in' speech. So have you told Sylvia how you feel?"

Garth shook his head in exasperation. "Have you gone deaf? I promised God I wouldn't have anything to do with her."

"And you think that's what He wants?" Matthew asked incredulously. "God doesn't make those kind of deals."

"Well, He made one with me. I had nothing else to offer."

"You didn't need to offer anything. God gives mercy, grace, forgiveness—they're free. You can't make deals for those kind of things."

"I can't?"

Matthew shook his head. "Let me explain how it works."

"This better be good."

Sylvia couldn't take it anymore. She had enough of her grandmother's Italian blood in her that she needed to cook when she was upset. The fact that she'd never learned to cook—never even learned when pasta was officially done—had stopped her for two days; but she woke up this morning and decided to make lasagna. After all, she reasoned, it was topped with mounds of mozzarella and anything topped with that much cheese had to taste good.

Besides, she remembered her grandmother not only chopping garlic and onions but also squeezing red Roma tomatoes to make the sauce. Sylvia suddenly wanted very much to chop something or squeeze something until it bled—even if it was only a vegetable.

What had ever possessed her to be such a fool as to actually believe she and that—that cold, insufferable man had anything between them? If he hadn't been so eager to fall in with Mrs. Buckwalter's scheme to teach the kids manners, he wouldn't have even paid any attention to her. He just needed a Ginger Rogers to play opposite his Fred Astaire. Some gentleman he turned out to be. He'd certainly gotten over the idea of courting her now that the dance was over. Just thinking about him made her want to get her hands on a ripe tomato and start to squeeze.

Garth paused outside the kitchen door and took off his Stetson. He slicked back his hair and bent his head in prayer. *Lord, Matthew better be right about your mercy. 'Cause I haven't got a chance without it.*

Garth looked at his reflection in the small square of half-frozen window to the side of the door. He looked a little scruffy. He wondered if he should go change before he went inside and made a fool of himself. Then he reasoned there was little point. Sylvia was always so much neater and composed than him that she wasn't likely to be impressed by his attire no matter what he wore. She hadn't even commented on the suit he'd borrowed from that Buckwalter fellow for the dance. And it was Italian.

Garth opened the kitchen door and his heart stopped.

It was dark inside the kitchen, but he could see clearly enough. Sylvia stood at the kitchen counter with tears running down her cheek and red splotches all over her clothes.

My God, she's bleeding!

"Where's the cut?" Garth demanded as he covered the space between the open door and the counter. Maybe the FBI was wrong. Maybe "the boss" wasn't headed to Mexico after all. "Who did this?"

Garth grabbed Sylvia's shoulders to steady her. She was looking at him as if she was disoriented, and he took action. The first thing they needed to guard against was fainting from loss of blood.

Sylvia knew what the girls meant when they said they could die from embarrassment. He was the last person she wanted to witness her humiliation. She'd taken on the vegetables and they had won. If she had her way, she'd turn and flee the kitchen, but she couldn't. He had her shoulders in a grip that didn't promise to let up anytime soon.

"Let's get you up on the counter," Garth said urgently. "That'll stop the blood flow."

"Oh, no, it's not—" Sylvia started to explain softly but it was too late. Garth's hands had found her waist and he hoisted her up on the counter and tipped her back until she was lying down in a bed of garlic peels and tomato pulp.

"Where does it hurt?" Garth demanded as he ran his hands over her stomach.

Sylvia drew in her breath involuntarily. She knew the kitchen was still cold. She could feel the ridges of cold pressed Formica against the back of her shoulders as she lay on the counter. But, even more keenly, she could feel the heat of Garth's hands through the cotton blouse she wore as he searched for a cut.

"It doesn't hurt—I didn't—"

"Don't be brave. I know it hurts."

"No." Sylvia took a deep breath. Why did she always seem short of breath when she was around him? "I'm not hurt. It's the tomatoes."

Garth smelled the tomato pulp at the same time as Sylvia spoke. Now he knew what the kids meant when they said they could die from embarrassment. "Sorry," he mumbled. "Reflex reaction, I guess."

Garth reluctantly took his hands away. Well, he'd certainly done it this time. Still, he looked a little closer—he rather liked Sylvia lying on her back looking up at him with a slightly dazed expression on her face. "You're sure it's only tomatoes?"

"I know it's a mess," Sylvia said stiffly. "I had no idea tomatoes could be so full of juice. But don't worry. I intend to clean the kitchen."

"I'm not worried about the kitchen."

"I was making lasagna."

"Lasagna sounds good." Garth reached down and pulled a paper towel off the roll inside the cabinet door. He couldn't help himself. He dabbed at the tomato on Sylvia's cheek.

"Well, there's not going to be lasagna now." Sylvia looked at him as if he was dense. "I never even got the sauce together."

"Something I can do to help?"

Sylvia looked at him as if he'd gotten even denser. "You?"

"I can cook," Garth protested. And then, to be more truthful, added "Well, we can cook."

His reward was a beautiful smile. Upside down and slightly out of focus. With tomato juice to one side. But it was the most beautiful smile he'd ever seen.

"Just like we can dance?" Sylvia teased.

"Hey, we made it around the floor." Garth arched out his arm like a gentleman so Sylvia could use it to pull herself upright. "I'm sure we can put together a lasagna."

Garth looked at the recipe in the cookbook. It talked about the preparation stage, the sauce stage, the assembly stage, the cooking stage and even the cooling stage. The only thing it didn't offer an opinion on was when in the whole process it was best to ask a very important, very personal question. He supposed it was the gentlemanly thing to do to wait until the cooking stage.

"It looks ready for the oven to me," Garth said as he eyed the two pans of lasagna they'd prepared.

"I'm just adding a little extra cheese."

Garth opened the oven door and grabbed a pot holder. "Just tell me when you're ready to move them."

Garth took a deep breath. He was close to the cooking stage and he needed a springboard before he took his dive. "Moving them," he continued. "That's the kind of heavy lifting thing that women like husbands around for—"

"Why?" Sylvia looked up, puzzled. "They're not that heavy."

"I didn't mean these in particular." Garth started to sweat. "I just meant in general. Husbands are good for lifting things. Heavy things."

"I have a dolly."

Lord, that mercy thing you have—maybe you could kick some in now. At least let me get the question out. "Well, of course, that's not the only thing husbands are good for—"

"I should hope not." Sylvia put the last of the cheese on the lasagnas and nodded toward the oven. "These are ready."

Garth took the reprieve and lifted the lasagnas into the oven before closing the door.

"It's set at three hundred and fifty degrees. That should be hot enough," Sylvia said as she reached behind herself to untie her apron. "I think I'll go change before I tackle this kitchen."

"Before you do, why don't you sit down a minute and answer my question?"

"What question?"

Garth decided he needed to sit down even if Sylvia didn't. "Well, I'm getting to that. Continuing our conversation and all."

"You have a question about lasagnas?" Sylvia asked as she sank down into a chair across the table from Garth. "You're more likely to find the answer in the recipe book."

"No, it's not about lasagnas. It's about husbands."

Garth watched Sylvia stiffen. His hopes plummeted.

"I know some people think every woman needs a husband to be complete, but I don't." Sylvia said the words succinctly.

"Well, of course, you don't need a husband." Garth was starting to sweat in earnest now. "My question was more along the lines of whether you wanted one."

"I can get a date if I need one." Sylvia's lips were pursed. "You don't need to set me up with anyone."

"I'm not trying to set you up." Garth ran his fingers through his hair.

"Well, then, what exactly is your question?"

Sylvia looked at him in a way that made him feel sympathy for an insect pinned to the pasteboard of some third grader's science project. Garth looked at the wall to his right. He looked to the wall to his left. He even looked up at the ceiling. He hadn't timed this right. There were no flowers. No violin music. Not even a smiling woman sitting across from him. He was dead.

"My question is 'Will you marry me?'" he said softly.

Sylvia looked at him in shock. "Marry you?"

The color drained from Sylvia's face and then rushed back in a flush as she looked behind her shoulder. "And who's listening to the lesson this time?"

"What?"

"Your lessons on how to charm women," Sylvia said sharply as she stood up. "I'm tired of being part of an object lesson that you use to try and teach these boys manners.''

''You think I'd want them to propose to someone just to show that they have the manners to pull it off?'' Garth was astonished. ''What kind of a fool do you think I am?''

Garth fumed about that question long after Sylvia left him sitting at the kitchen table. He hadn't really expected her to throw her arms around him and say yes when he asked her, but he'd certainly expected to be taken seriously. Instead, she'd stood up and run from the kitchen as if he had the plague.

Maybe I do have the plague, he thought to himself glumly as he cleaned the kitchen. Even God's mercy didn't help him get a respectable answer. He wondered what Matthew would have to say about that. Ah well, there was cleaning to do. He took his sponge and wiped off the back of the stove. There was even tomato pulp on the salt shaker. He didn't know Sylvia was standing in the doorway until he heard a little surprised squeak.

''I didn't think you'd still be here,'' Sylvia said. She'd obviously taken a shower and washed the tomato pulp out of her hair. ''It's my mess. You don't have to clean it up.''

''I don't mind.''

Sylvia took a deep breath. She'd changed into a clean peach-colored blouse. She'd put on light peach lipstick and curled her hair. But she still didn't feel as poised as she'd like. Garth had rattled her and she'd reacted badly.

''I need to apologize,'' she began stiffly.

"No, you don't."

"It's just—I was a mess."

"There's no need to apologize. I'm sorry if I took you by surprise."

Sylvia bit her lip. She felt suddenly very lost. "It's just—whatever gave you that idea to propose?"

Garth looked at her and smiled, warm and lazy like a long summer afternoon. For the first time since she'd started squeezing tomatoes, Sylvia felt her soul lighten.

"I've had that particular idea for some time now. Maybe since that day I pulled you out of that snow-drift."

"You mean, you're serious?" Sylvia watched his eyes.

"Of course I'm serious," Garth said as he stepped closer. She'd forgotten how his eyes darkened and his lips turned up in a private half smile. "I wouldn't have asked you to marry me if I wasn't serious about it."

"But why?"

Garth stepped even closer and this time he cuddled a hand under her chin. "You're the love of my life. I'd like nothing better than spending the rest of my life with you."

"But I have all these kids—" Sylvia stalled. She needed to think. *Dear Lord, was he serious?*

Garth shrugged. "I've got plenty of room for kids."

"You're serious?" Sylvia repeated. The squeezing inside of her stomach was being replaced by a warm glowing heat. Garth wanted to marry her.

"I've never been more serious about anything in my life."

Sylvia looked at him. She'd become an excellent judge of the twitches that gave away kids who were lying. All she saw in Garth's eyes was a steady, un-flinching sincerity.

"Are you going to ask me again?"

Garth smiled. "Try and stop me."

Sylvia smiled, too. Then Garth dipped his head and kissed her. Garth's kiss ran through her like a kick and ended up like bells in her ears. No, wait a minute, that was—

"—lasagna," Sylvia muttered as she pulled away from Garth. "The lasagna's done."

The kitchen timer was impatiently ringing.

"Mmm, it can cook a minute or two longer," Garth murmured as he nuzzled her ear. "First, I want to hear your answer to my proposal."

"You haven't even said if you love me yet."

"I love you more than life," Garth said simply. "I'm not perfect and I know you deserve a man who is more devout than me even though Matthew says all men start out from the same place with God—"

"He's right on that one," Sylvia said.

"I do promise you," Garth continued, "that as long as God gives me breath, you can always count on the fact that I'll do my best to love Him and love you."

Sylvia watched his face. The face of her beloved. She could spend a lifetime learning to know his face.

"Then the answer is yes," she whispered. "Yes, yes, yes!"

Epilogue

A month or so later

Sylvia and Garth had thirty flower bearers for their wedding—each one of the kids wanted to carry a bouquet of roses and Mrs. Buckwalter promised Robert would personally fly in dozens of roses from the flower marts in Denver. Mrs. Buckwalter gave Robert special directions on how to pick out the best of the pink roses and the freshest of the white roses and the most perfectly shaped of the ivory ones. Finally she offered to go with him to see that he did it right.

Robert assured his mother that he ran two Fortune 500 companies; he could see to some roses. Mrs. Buckwalter didn't listen. She sent Jenny with him.

As for Sylvia, she blanched when she realized how many roses were being planned. She pointed out that the money could provide for another teenager or two. Mrs. Buckwalter paid her no attention.

"It's your wedding day, my dear," the older woman said as though that explained everything.

And maybe it did, Sylvia thought.

As for Garth, he had only one request for the wedding. He wanted to surprise Sylvia with fresh preaches. He had Jenny help him place an order for a truckload of fresh spring peaches. Their odor filled the barn with summer and Sylvia smiled as she walked down the aisle.

* * * * *

Dear Reader,

I hope you enjoyed the story of Sylvia and Garth. I wanted to show a woman who—like most of us—has struggled with fear in her relationships. It would have been easy for Sylvia to listen only to those fears. But, in doing so, she'd have missed out on the gift of love Garth was offering.

If you have similar fears in your life, I pray you will not let them stop you from accepting the love of others, whether it be the love of a friend, a family member, or the love of that special man. In the beginning of the book, I chose the words of *Isaiah* 14:3 to remind us that God can give us rest from our fears. Once our fears have been put to rest, we can accept the gift of love and friendship others have for us.

May we all love well and fearlessly.

Janet Tronstad